THE ONE YOU CHOSE

A Ridgewood Holiday Novella

LINNEA MARCH

To Heidi, who loves the holiday season
Rusty for being my forever New Year's kiss
and to Sluy's Bakery for creating doughboys

CONTENTS

EXACTLY TWELVE O'CLOCK

Lina

W ithout fail, the Wednesday before Thanksgiving felt like a high school reunion. The Skol House was packed to its chipped paint and neon beer sign brim. Hard cider was spilled, two different couples had a screeching fight in front of a closed Sluy's bakery and one person had attempted to climb onto the second-floor balcony of Prost Euro-Pub to fall and sprain their ankle. The air smelled of beer, salt air, and sweat. The town was in full revelry and I was not having a good time.

"So, it's like that coupon you get at Old Navy when you spend fifty dollars?" I raised my brow innocently at the guy in front of me.

He blinked a few times as he processed my sentence. "What? No, they are nothing alike..."

I interrupted, "from the way you're describing it, it sounds like this crypto-currency is exactly like that." I took a sip of my craft beer and waited for the guy to either explain again or walk away. Despite knowing better, I was hoping for the latter. This was the problem with small-town bars during the holidays. It was always a complete shit show. Every school crush from seventh grade was shooting her shot. Every hot-shot baseball player was recalling his glory days. The *remember when* and the *you'll never guess who I just saw* stories that blended into the mediocre music the DJ played.

I already had three separate conversations with three different ex-boyfriends about what they were doing. Including my crypto-currency-obsessed junior prom date, who somehow was still trying to explain digital currency to me. He couldn't take the hint when we were sixteen and it didn't look like he got any more sense in the eight years since then. I waited for him to finish his diatribe, before shrugging my shoulder. "I don't see the difference."

As the guy walked away in a huff, likely off to harangue some other unsuspecting girl, I fidgeted around in this mistake of a short red dress. My roommate, Zoya, was at least four inches shorter than me and had a lot more up top to fill out. Why I let her talk me into wearing this outfit, I had no idea, but after the third tequila shot we took at the apartment before heading out it seemed like a good idea. Now I was left resting my elbow on a tall table while Zoya chatted with her boyfriend, Milo.

Tonight was supposed to be my first date with Chad, the uncle of one of my students at the preschool. When he asked me for my number after trick or treating with his niece, I said no. Dating a family member of a student wasn't exactly against the rules, but in a small town, it wasn't a smart choice. As cute as he was, he didn't exude the qualities that would be worth my job for a single date.

But I'll give him this. He was persistent. Suddenly, he was there every Thursday afternoon picking up his niece and asking for my number. Three weeks of it and I relented, half to get him to stop asking while I was elbows deep in oobleck and half because I was curious if he'd manage to live up to all this big talk.

So I agreed to dinner at the local tapas restaurant. I figured even if he was a bust, they had a tasty house sangria. Only to have him bail on me. After I did my make-up. So here I am, red dress on, straps of my heels digging painfully into my ankle. Annoyed.

Across the bar, I caught sight of Matt Hansen. In high school, he had been a big deal but had since been divorced when he got his ex-wife's best friend pregnant. The best friend and the baby didn't live in Ridgewood anymore, but everyone knew what happened. Matt held his beer up at me and gave one of those ridiculous chin nods guys gave. I never understood how they thought that looked cool. Looking around, I hoped that there was someone else Matt was nodding at. No such luck. I made the mistake of holding his gaze a second too long and he started walking towards me. Damn.

Deciding I had better flee before I got caught being hit on by Matt, I ducked behind a pillar, clutching my drink to my chest. The line for the back door was a clear shot. I moved, walking sideways through the throngs of people dancing to old-school hip-hop, and made it out the back door where all the smokers congregated too close to the door.

Closing my eyes, I rested my head against the cold metal wall. The mixture of tequila and craft beer swirled through my stomach. I could be in bed right now, comfortable pajamas on, my favorite teen drama about witches playing while I cut out the paper salmons for the color-matching game for my students. Instead, Zoya dragged me out of the house. It didn't matter that there were far more people in town this weekend, nights in the Ridgewood bar were all the same. Life in Ridgewood was the same.

Truly, I loved my hometown. Far enough from Seattle to not worry about crime, but close enough that we still had a good grocery store. I loved Freedom Bay and the fireworks over the Fjord every summer. The barista at my favorite coffee drive-through stand who would start making my drink when she saw my car. Ridgewood was great, nevertheless, I wanted something, anything, more. I should have gone to college somewhere farther away. Volunteered for the Peace Corps or something. Nothing was keeping me here. Except for all my friends, my family, and the way no one could make a better pizza than Ridgewood Market.

Was this a quarter-life crisis? Every morning I would get up and think, maybe this will be the day things will click and I'll figure out what the next step was for me. I had a job I loved that paid me an insanely low wage for my labor, but that was on the education industry. A cute apartment and a few friends. But it was all the same. I sighed heavily, resting my head against the wall. The late November wind whipped at my ankles and I cursed Zoya again for making me wear this outfit. Wrapping my jacket tighter around myself, I glanced at the alley. If I timed it right, I could be home in fifteen minutes and still catch the evening news.

"You doing okay?" a deep melodic voice asked. Startled, I stepped out from the wall to look at the man attached to the voice and found my words dying in my throat. In front of me was the most gorgeous man I had ever seen. Golden-skinned with warm brown eyes that seemed to pierce right through me. He had thick curls I wanted to feel under my fingers. He was taller than me, even with my heels, putting him over six feet. His full lips quirked a smile at me, repeating the question.

"Uh, yeah," I mumbled. *Smooth talker, Lina.* My hands suddenly felt very damp and gross. "I just needed some fresh air. It was getting crowded in there."

"Is it always this busy?" he asked, peering into the open door where the DJ switched from the 90s hip-hop song to an 80s girl anthem. A piercing "woo" went up as twenty girls rushed the dance floor and every man disappeared to the edges.

Looking back at him, I shook my head. "Not on a Wednesday night, no. It's because of the holiday. With everyone home to visit their parents, they're making up for months of being professional adults by binge drinking and chatting up their middle school crush before they sit down at their grandmother's house for pumpkin pie tomorrow."

"Is that what you're hiding from? Your middle school crush?" The man asked.

I darted my eyes from the back door where Matt Hanson was now talking to a pretty redhead. He was certainly one to subscribe to the *A Bird in the Hand is Worth Two in the Bush* type philosophy for picking up women. "Not my crush, no."

"But you are hiding?"

Grabbing the end of my ponytail, I tugged at my hair, a nervous habit I'd been trying for years to kick. "Hiding is such a strong word. Looking for a brief reprieve? Evading the throng."

"Circumventing the crowd?" He asked, the corner of his mouth hitching up to expose an almost dimple. I wondered what that dimple would feel like under my finger. Or lips.

I nodded, "Yes, exactly."

"The crowd, or someone in particular?" He stepped closer. In the streetlight I could see he was wearing a maroon flannel shirt over a tee shirt with art I recognized from a recent art exhibit in Seattle.

"Both. Neither. It's kind of a high school reunion in there and I'm not really in the mood to reminisce about the time I tripped on stage during a fashion show and had to get five stitches on my chin." Without thinking, I ran a finger over that scar. It took years of expensive creams to smooth the keloid down.

"Well, I can tell you I know nothing about your fashion show blunders or anything else about high school in Ridgewood. This is my first time here at..." He glanced over his shoulder at the metal back door festooned with bumper stickers, furrowing his brow. "What's this place called again?"

"Skol House. Skol like *cheers*, not like a skeleton." In the air, I mimicked someone toasting a beer. My cheeks felt warm, and I ran my hands over the front of my dress, drying them as best I could. "They like a good Nordic theme around here."

"I'm learning that. I've only been here in town for a few weeks, but I have noticed there are a lot more Viking helmets for sale than in your average place." He grinned and I felt my knees get weak. He had a perfect row of straight white teeth. Reflexively I smiled back at him, hoping my red lipstick hadn't faded to only the outline of my lips the way it always seemed to. He put his hand out. "Fitz."

Putting my hand in his, a zip of energy traveled up my arm, warming my insides and other neglected areas I couldn't focus on yet. Sucking in a breath, I fought to compose myself. "Lina."

The street light above us blanched my skin. Fitz held on to my hand for a while. I had the sense he might bring my hand to his lips and kiss the back of my hand like those historical dramas I loved to watch when I was sick. His thumb traced the skin there before dropping my hand and my skin tingled from the contact.

That's interesting.

"Are you having a good time, Lina?" His mouth wrapped around my name like a prayer.

"Can I be honest?" I asked. When Fitz nodded, I breathed out loudly. "I'm not. My friend Zoya talked me into wearing these shoes after three shots of tequila. I couldn't feel my toes then, but I can feel them now."

Gritting my teeth, I decided I was done for the night. Chad was a bust, creepy Matt Hanson was a bust and I certainly wasn't going to find any more happiness wearing these shoes. I rested my back against the garage door, lifting one foot up and pulling the strappy heel off. Setting my bare foot on the ground, I repeated the motion with my other foot. Fitz watched as if transfixed by the movements. Something about the way he watched me as I moved made me feel like I was removing more than just my shoes. I liked the thrum of excitement his look gave me.

"So let's get out of here." He blinked at me as if he was as surprised by the words as I was. He held out his hand. "Do you want to?"

I thought about laughing. Any sane person would in that scenario. This guy was a stranger in my small town. I watched enough true crime to know this was exactly the way to end up weighed down by a cement block in the middle of Freedom Bay and having Keith Morrison saying I lit up every room I walked into. Which would be emphatically false.

Opening my mouth to decline, I found myself doing the opposite. Nodding, I wordlessly took his hand, lacing my fingers with his. Marveling at the softness of his palm and the callouses on his fingertips. Our hands fit together perfectly.

Inside my chest, it was as if a wave washed through me. His hand in mine. The quiet assurance of his strong grip of my palm. The way he looked at me. I didn't know what this feeling was coursing through me. All I knew was I wanted to feel that way again. An implacable calm overtook me. I would go home with this man. He was different. I would be different. If only for the night.

He took the shoes out of my hand and looped the strap over a finger, letting them dangle from his other hand. As I followed behind him, my body warmed with anticipation.

I kept telling myself I wasn't the sort of girl who did this. Never had I left the bar with a guy, much less one that I only met minutes before. I couldn't do hookups. This wasn't the anonymity of Seattle. This was Ridgewood, where my doctor also lived next door to my parents. Where when I was caught making out with my high school boyfriend behind the junior high, the cops called my parents before I returned home. I knew most of the men my age in Ridgewood, except for the military guys from the nearby naval base that filtered through the bar and then were gone months later.

Fitz was neither of these things. His hair was too long to be in the service. He held himself differently. He was like nothing I had ever seen before.

I knew it could all be a mistake, but damnit, I was canceled on by a guy I didn't want to date. My hair looked good and this beautiful man was standing in front of me, wanting me. I might never identify exactly what it was inside me that told me to take this chance. For the first time in my life, I went blindly into the night.

FONDLY KISSING

Lina

In Ridgewood, there was the Freedom Bay Resort, down by the water and costing hundreds of dollars a night. It boasted a full-service spa, room service, and summer concerts. Then there were the Ridgewood Inn and Suites, which had none of those things. As a teenager, we used to sneak into the hot tub of the inn. The fence around the pool had a faulty lock that all the teenagers knew how to open. You had to time it just right to get past the night security guard. A year after I left high school, the inn finally upgraded the lock to one that required a room key. My deprived younger brother never got to experience the joy of sneaking in.

Standing behind him, I waited as he unlocked one of the many blank doors in a long row facing the main road. "You live in the hotel?"

"It's an extended stay place, and it's just for a few more days. My rental won't be ready until the first. I promise I don't plan on living out of a hotel room for long."

He shot me a warm smile over his shoulder as he pulled the door open. As he glanced away into the hotel room, I pulled my phone out and shot a quick text to Zoya that if I was murdered; it was the guy in room 209 of the Ridgewood Inn and Suites.

"Sending your friend your location?" He smirked at me and my nether bits tingled.

"No, I was..." Damn, I never could lie.

"It's okay. You have to stay safe, right? I can get my driver's license out if you want a picture of that, too." His eyes were genuine. I could tell he wasn't making fun of me and that his offer only solidified my decision.

I tried to squash the smile that was forming. "No, that's okay."

"The offer stands." Fitz turned all the lights on in the hotel room as we entered. Glancing around, I saw the room was in disarray. There were still dishes in the sink and his clothes were piled in a chair beside the bed.

"Sorry if I had known I'd have company I'd of done the dishes," he paused, glancing at the chair. "And put the clothes away."

My eyes caught on the suitcase on the floor. "You're living in a hotel room, all alone over Thanksgiving weekend."

"When you say it like that." Scratching a spot on his jaw with his thumbnail, he looked sheepish. "My Ma is on a girl's trip to Tulum for the weekend. After Pops passed, we don't really make a big fuss about Thanksgiving. Christmas is where she goes all out."

I opened my mouth, about to invite him to my parent's house the next day, then closed it. That was not a one-night stand conversation. That was a three-month dating conversation. Six months of dating? In truth, I had no idea. What I knew was, I couldn't ask this guy I just met to meet my family. My terrible Uncle Chester, who would spend the entire afternoon asking people their thoughts on the latest diet craze. Or cousin Josie, who liked to practice her new Judo moves out on unsuspecting males. If there was a one-night stand handbook, that had to be on the first page.

Changing the subject, I walked further into his hotel room, glancing around. "I love this time of year. There's something special about the holidays. But I think my favorite is New Year's Eve. The changing into a new year, another chance to make something of yourself, a chance to create more, to fall in love, to learn about the world. The idea of a fresh start."

As Fitz stared at me, I felt as if his warm eyes were seeing right into the very center of me. I hoped he liked what he saw. He stepped closer to me, his eyes darting down to my lips. I could sense how his lips would taste on mine. Taking a step back, I looked away. Not quite ready yet.

"Um, can I get you a drink?" Fitz asked, opening the mini fridge under the counter. Inside was a pizza box, beer, and a small bottle of a popular hot sauce.

"That's quite a stash you have there." I motioned to the fridge. "Very balanced diet."

Fitz pulled out the hot sauce, shaking it in his hand. "I don't go anywhere without this. It goes good on everything."

Shaking my head, I pulled the hot sauce out of his hand to examine it. "That stuff is trash. You need some sriracha. That's the good stuff."

"False. Incorrect. I won't hear it." Fitz swiped the small bottle out of my hand and clutched it to his chest. "Mine is way hotter."

I shook my head. "No way. I bet they're the same on the Scoville scale. But mine had better flavor."

"Look at you pulling out the pepper verbiage."

"And look at you getting defensive about your hot sauce." I teased.

Narrowing his eyes, he looked me up and down. "Do you want a drink, or are you going to keep giving me a hard time about my superior choice in hot sauce?"

Laughing, I sat on the edge of the bed. "I'll take a drink."

"Alright." He set the hot sauce back in its place and scanned the contents of the fridge. "I have water and an orange juice that I opened a few days and should probably have tossed out and um... a rhubarb beer someone gave me when I started my job."

I wrinkled my nose. "A water would be fine. I know that rhubarb beer. The local brewery always makes it in the springtime. No one likes it, so it's always discounted. They keep bringing it back every year, though."

Fitz handed me the glass of water. As I took a small sip, I looked around the room for a place to set the glass. Fitz reached out to take the glass from me. His fingers brushed mine and sparks tingled up my arm at the contact. Raising my eyes to him. His whiskey-brown gaze warmed me the same as if I was sipping a single malt. I pulled my hands away, folding them in my lap.

I glanced down at my hands, still tingling from his contact. "I know this sounds cliche, but I've never done this before. Going home with a guy I just met. It's not just talk, I swear. I've lived here my whole life and I know all the guys my age."

Fitz placed the glass down on the bedside table and sat beside me. "I know it's not talk. I can tell." He reached between us and took my hand. I marveled at how our fingers laced together, the softness of his palm. "We don't have to do anything. I can call you a ride if you don't feel comfortable."

I shook my head. "No. I don't want that. I'm comfortable and want this. It's like..." I bit off the last of my statement. How could I tell him that when he emerged from the shadows, something passed over me, telling me to trust where the night with this man would take me? I'd sound crazy. I felt crazy. Watching his hand, I marveled at how our fingers fit together. He flipped my hand over, palm up, and drew a circle with his finger. "You're going to think I'm insane."

"Try me." He assured me.

"Do you believe in signs?"

"I don't know, I've never thought about it."

"Well, I don't. Or I didn't. But earlier today I was going to go on a date with a guy who ended up canceling at the last minute. I wanted to stay home, but my friend Zoya said I shouldn't waste my fancy hair and make-up. So, I go out and I see you then I..."

As he reached forward to tuck a wisp of hair that had fallen out of my ponytail behind my ear, a zing of energy coursed through me at his contact. "You don't have to explain it. I understand."

Blinking, I stared at him. "You do?"

Nodding he, leaned forward, cupping my cheek in his hand. "You know what I thought when I first saw you?"

Shaking my head, I kept my eyes on him. His thumb brushed against my cheekbone, his fingers resting just behind my ear and in my hair. "I need to know her."

My voice a whisper, I stared up at him. "I wanted to know you, too."

"Not want. Need. I needed to know you."

"You're not lying, are you? Because I can handle the truth, but I can't do liars. That's my deal breaker, no-go thing."

He shook his head. "No, I'm not lying. I'm feeling a lot of things right now, but everything I'm feeling right now is true." He dipped his face closer, his words a hush over me. "I'm going to kiss you now. If you don't want me to, you need to say so."

"Kiss me." My eyes fluttered shut. "Please."

His hand gripped the back of my neck, pulling my face to his. His lips were soft against my own, a gentle pressure as he tentatively kissed me. Bringing my hand up to his shoulder, I wrapped my arms around him, pulling him closer. The long lines of his body pressed against the soft curves of me. His fingers under my hair, tracing a line on my back down to the zipper of my dress. I shrugged out of my coat, discarding it on the floor beside us. Everywhere he touched was sparking under my skin. We tumbled back onto the bed. His hands on my bare leg, my lips on his neck. He settled between my thighs, my dress riding up my legs until he was at the center of me. His firm length pushed against my clit.

"How are you this soft?" His words against the hollow of my throat. Savoring the tremors wracking my body, I wrapped my legs around his waist, pulling him closer.

"I need to feel you."

Deep inside the chambers on my chest, I felt a part of myself blooming. All I wanted was his touch, the feel of his back under my nails, and the rasp of his breath on my skin.

Every caress, every shared breath repeated; this is right, this is home.

GOOD AND TIGHT

Fitz

How could anyone be so soft?

Lina's skin under my hands, I reveled in the feel of her. There was no way I could have known when I was dragged out by my new coworkers that this was the way my night would end.

Going out to the bar hadn't been my scene since my days in college, but when my coworkers had guilt-tripped me into coming out, I couldn't find a good reason to stay in the aging hotel room for another night. Since arriving in town a week before, I had spent most of my nights eating takeout and going to bed at nine.

What my coworkers failed to mention was that it was the only bar open in town on a holiday weekend. It was full of young twenty-somethings drinking Jaeger bombs and shouting over loud music. I had only been there for five minutes before I regretted my choice. I could tell that this was a local scene and having someone new in the bar was causing people to notice. Girls that looked like they were fifteen kept eying me, one even sending over a beer. I tried to be gracious but firm. While I appreciated the drink, I wasn't interested. As nice as the girls looked, I had moved to the town only a week before. Settling into my job at the humane society and setting up my new place needed to be my priority over getting my dick wet. Besides, this wasn't Seattle. I had never lived in a town this small before, but I had the feeling if I slept with a girl here, everyone would know. And my new co-worker, Cooper, seemed like the worst kind of gossip there was. Whoever said men don't gossip hadn't met this man. One drink into the night and I already heard the tragic back story of at least four different classmates. Did I really need to know that Sasha by the bathroom got in a snowmobile accident at sixteen and had to get plastic surgery? No, but I knew it now.

One more drink, that's what I told myself. I'd finish this beer and have one more, then I could walk back to the inn and suites where a cold slice of pizza and my favorite hot sauce were waiting for me.

Then Lina walked in.

I felt a shock run through my body. The sight of this woman ravaged me. My whole uneventful life had led me to this moment where she stood with her back to me. I knew her. She was the girl I had been waiting for. I needed to talk to her.

The way her dark ponytail swung behind her, so long it brushed the back of her elbows. Her willowy frame in that red dress. The way she walked uncomfortably behind her friend. I noticed the other men in the bar watching her, too. As she talked with various people, there was a tightness to her mouth, even when she was smiling at them. Couldn't anyone else see it? She wanted to be at that bar even less than I did.

When she moved away from her table, her tiny purse in hand, I had the overwhelming desire to follow behind her.

I wasn't typically so bold. I couldn't remember the last time I struck up a conversation with a complete stranger before. But something about the girl drew me closer until I stood in front of her.

I had no idea what came over me to invite her back to my place. She could be one of those black widow killers for all I knew. But at that moment, all I wanted was to feel her hand on mine as I walked her back to my hotel room.

Now she was here and her coat was falling off her shoulders and I could run my hands down her soft arms.

Her lips found mine. She tasted of sweet mint. Her tongue traced the seam of my lips and I opened for her. My hands traced down her bare back until I got to the zipper of her dress. Never leaving her kiss, I eased the zipper down. I didn't know why she wore such a small dress in late November, but I was happy to pull the thin straps off her shoulder, baring her warm skin. Breaking our kiss, my mouth trailed down her throat. Lina tilted her head back, moaning as my mouth moved from her throat to her collarbone. As I kissed the bare skin of her shoulder, she pushed my flannel off my shoulders. I pulled away, grabbing the back of my tee shirt and pulling it over my head in a quick motion.

"Damn, that was so hot." Lina was breathing heavily as she watched me. She raised a hand to my bare chest, running a finger over my nipple. Catching my eye, she smiled. "Do you have any idea how hot that move is?"

My fingers found the bodice of her dress, pulling it down until it pooled around her waist. "Tell me."

A wicked gleam in her eye, she tucked her thumbs into the sides of her dress, pulling it down until it fell to the floor. Clad in only tiny lace, her body took my breath away. Every inch of her skin was smooth. Her breasts were the perfect size to fit in my hand and her hips flared out just enough to grab onto. A thin line of slightly darker hair trailed from her belly button to under the lace underwear. She was perfect.

As she leaned back on the bed, her tits stretched against the fabric, begging to be let loose.

"That's some, uhhh." I motioned to her lingerie. "Lacy stuff."

"I told you. I had a date tonight."

"And you were going to let him see this?" A surge of possessiveness took over me. I barely knew this woman. I didn't even know her last name yet, and this wasn't the time to ask. But it didn't matter. Staring at her golden silk skin, I wanted to be the last man who would see her like this. I wanted to be the only.

"No, I told you. I don't do this. I only wore it for a little confidence boost."

I ran a finger over the top of her left breast, pulling her bra down to expose her bud. "And do you feel confident?"

Before she could answer me, I bent down, taking one brown nipple into my mouth. A moan sounded as I swirled my tongue around the hard nub. Her hands buried in my hair, securing me to her chest as I sucked and teased. She wrapped her legs around me, bringing my hard dick against her center.

"Take off your pants. I want to feel you." She demanded.

I made short work of removing my pants and boxers, before grabbing a condom out of my suitcase. There were only three left. I wasn't expecting to hook up with anyone, but I had a feeling we'd run through them all by the end of the night.

"Good goddamn." She watched me, her eyes raking down my body like she was hungry for it. I had never been the most devoted gym member, opting for daily runs more for my mental health than fitness, under her eyes, I felt like the hottest man in the world. Her eyes left my hard cock to look at my eyes. She pulled off her underwear, throwing them to the side. "Get over here."

Propping myself up on my arms above her, our bodies fit together. I kissed her deeply, my hard cock begging to be inside her, but I couldn't. Not yet.

Sliding down her body, I kneeled on the floor in front of her. I ran a hand up her legs, pulling her knees apart until I was level with her cunt. As I kissed a line up her inner thigh, her hands came to rest on my hair, her short nails scraping against me. With one finger I parted her, the slickness of her wetting my finger. Plunging a finger inside her then two, I moved my hand against her. She moaned and I sped up. My thumb traced a circle around her clit and she let out an "oh my god" and I pressed harder. Three fingers inside her, I leaned forward, lapping at her slit as I pumped inside her.

"That's right, come all over my hand." I coaxed before sucking her clit into my mouth. I swirled my tongue around it until I could feel her tense around my fingers.

She cried out, loud enough that I was sure I'd get a complaint the next day. I didn't care. While she was still coming down from her climax, I slid the condom down my length.

The moment I pushed inside her, I knew I was fucked. Nothing felt as good as her pussy around my cock. Reaching around her body, I pulled her up to sit on my lap. Her legs wrapped around my waist as I moved her above me. As she threw her head back, I took one nipple in my mouth, sucking it as I played with her other nipple. She ground herself against me. Pumping fast, I knew I couldn't last long. I just had to give her one more orgasm before I spent myself. The same stuttering cry she had before began and I moved faster, dragging my teeth against her tender flesh, and then I felt her contracting around me. I came right after her, holding on tight as the orgasm ripped through me. Our bodies slick with sweat, her arms wrapped around me tight, keeping me inside her.

"Oh God, oh." She murmured over and over as her body slowly relaxed into me.

Pulling away I smoothed the little hair that fell from her ponytail from her face.

"Yeah?"

A smile brightened her face. "Yeah."

Adjusting myself, I laid us down, side by side on the bed. One leg still around my hips and her face inches from mine.

"Stay, tonight, will you?" I asked. Already I was picturing the next day. Maybe I'd find a twenty-four-hour breakfast place. I'd feed her food and then we'd come back here and do all this over again.

In the back of my mind, I realized tomorrow was Thanksgiving. She'd likely want to spend the day with her family and I certainly wouldn't invite myself over, but I'd claim her morning, and then we'd make plans for the rest of the long weekend. I opened my mouth to ask her but she snuggled in closer to my bare chest, her dark hair fanning out over her shoulders. I didn't want to ruin this moment. That was a tomorrow conversation. I had a feeling we'd have plenty of tomorrows.

ONE LITTLE CHANCE

Lina

I should have known that it was going to be a long day. Until my mother called and woke me up that morning, I had completely forgotten about the turkey trot fun run my father signed the whole family up for. I was more of a few cocktails to get the holidays started type girl. Not the jogging in an orange tutu and turkey hat at 9 am in the few degrees above freezing rain type girl. After a recent health scare, my parents were going over the top in making fitness fun. I was signed up against my will. The only solace I had was that my 17-year-old cousin Jason would also be woken up to do the run. Seeing him in a turkey hat beside his mother, my Aunt Cathy, made the concept easier.

Three blocks into my walk to my car I wondered if I should have woken up Fitz. Something, anything. I was so disoriented when my phone woke me all I could do was get that ridiculous dress on and find my purse. I could see groups of people grouped together near the start of the race. An oversized sign with a turkey and Viking both clad in horned helmets and running shorts hung over Front Street. Pulling out my phone to check the time I saw I had fifteen text messages from Zoya ranging from excited, bewildered, and nervous. I sent her a quick message that I was fine, hungover, and now doing the fun run with my family. I knew she wouldn't be getting up until noon today, anyway.

Stopping by my car, parked behind Sticky Cow brewery, I snagged my gym bag out of the trunk before making my way to my family huddled together. Despite rarely using the gym, I kept the bag in the car more for wishful thinking than anything.

"You can't run in that dress," my mother said, her hand over her heart. Lowering her voice, she bent down close. "Evangelina Grace McConnell, your cha-cha is hanging out for everyone to see."

Suppressing the impulse to groan, I leaned forward to press a kiss on my mother's cheek. "Thank you Mom, for saying that." I held up the gym bag. "I have my stuff right here. But if you want me to stay back, I can..."

"No, no. Your father is just begging for an excuse to get out of this. Don't you dare. Go into the bathroom to change. Don't touch the toilet seat, you know there's all sorts of nasties on that." My mother shoved a travel pack of wet wipes in my hands. "And wipe yourself down, you smell like a bar. I'll wait for you."

Sweaty, I pulled my hair out of its day-old ponytail that likely smelled like sex and beer. In the metal mirror I plaited my hair to help the ridiculous hat fit over my head. My threadbare sports bra kept getting stuck on my sticky skin. Finally wrangling on the tight pants I looked at my reflection. Mascara smeared, my skin shades lighter than normal. The burnt orange color of the race tee-shirt did nothing for my complexion. I looked haggard. Was this a Thanksgiving event or Halloween? I wasn't hungover. Wasn't *that* hungover. I looked like I just had a one-night stand. My mother might not recognize it on me, but I felt like there was an enormous banner over my head that said *Freshly f'd. Just had three orgasms from a guy I just met. Didn't even get his last name!*

I didn't regret the choice to sleep with Fitz. If anything, I wished I could have had more experiences like that before so I wouldn't have been so awkward. I never dated someone I hadn't known for years before. I had exactly five and a half boyfriends in my life. Had slept with three of them. Small towns weren't known for allowing the anonymity of one-night stands. Maybe if I had slept with a few more guys, I would have known what the protocol for such a thing was.

A bang on the door and a yell to "get your ass in gear" from my dad, and I was off. Turkey hat and all.

An hour and a half later, I finished the race with my family. They took a slew of pictures where my eyes were no doubt half closed, that my aunt would post every single one in a Facebook album.

As I got into my car, I rested my head back and squeezed my eyes shut, the headache that had been threatening me all morning forming along my temples. I was thankful for the quick moments of respite before I would meet up with everyone back at my parent's. My family would start drinking or cooking depending on their own skill set. There would be arguments over how much onion to use in the stuffing and what kind of cranberry sauce was best. I preferred the canned kind you can slice by the indent. It would be loud, warm, and overwhelming.

Driving past the Ridgewood Inn and Suites, I considered what I should do about Fitz. Pausing at the red light, I considered what would be more awkward, going back and knocking on his door to give him my number? Or just leaving it? We didn't discuss what would happen the night before. Wasn't leaving the next morning what you did? Scrubbing a hand over my grimy face I cursed myself. How could I be almost in my mid-twenties and not know this stuff? There was no way he was still sleeping. I didn't have a key to his room. I would have to knock on his door, and then what? Have an awkward conversation where he obviously wasn't interested.

But if he was... my thumb traced the line of my bottom lip, remembering the way his lips felt against mine. And then the ways those lips felt against my stomach and my breasts and my...

I didn't even get the guy's last name and yet I had more of a connection with him than the boys I dated before. Boys I had shared juice boxes with in the school cafeteria. Boys that sang beside me in jazz choir and tried to feel me up in the hallway after school dances. Boys who had no idea how to use their hands and lips. And tongues.

The car behind me laid on its horn, jolting me out of my thought process. Fighting the urge to flip off the driver behind me, I drove straight up the hill and away from the Inn. He was there until the first. I could find my courage by then, right?

BELLS ALL RING

Fitz

G roggy, I rolled over to the middle of the bed, my hand straying to find Lina only to find nothing but cold starched sheets. Opening one eye I saw her side of the bed was empty. I raised my head to look around the small room. Her glass of water still sitting beside the small sink, my clothes in a heap on the floor. All my stuff was here, but Lina was gone. Flopping back I stared up at the ceiling. Why didn't I get her number last night, and ask her to stay? Something.

The last one-night stand I had was on vacation, a nothing fling, but we agreed to it being a nothing. I realized I talked to that woman far more about my expectations than I did Lina. How could Lina know I wanted her to stay when I never asked her?

There was a loud knock on the door and I rolled out of bed, scrambling to find my pants. Maybe it was Lina coming back from getting ice or something. Maybe she got us coffee. Envisioning her on the other side, I left my shirt off.

When I opened up, an older gentleman with a Ridgewood Inn and Suites name tag with the name Walter, stood in the doorway. "Sorry to bother you, Mr. Deir."

I bit back a groan, smiling at him. "No bother. How can I help you, Walter?"

Walter folded his hands together and frowned. "We're having some plumbing issues in the room beside yours. We'll need to shut off the water for this block of rooms until the issue is resolved. The hotel was hoping we could ask you to move to another room for a bit. We'll help with the move if you'd like, I can bring you a cart, and we'll comp you a night."

I glanced back at my sparse room. Most of my stuff was in storage until the house was ready on the first. A break on a single night would be helpful for my wallet. Prices in Ridgewood were cheaper than Seattle, but they weren't cheap. "Okay. I can do that."

Closing the door, I took stock of the empty room.

The room looked exactly the same, but I was different. Irrevocably changed. On the bedside table was her water from the night before. I picked it up, the glass cold in my hand. There was a smudge of red lipstick on the rim. Rubbing the imprint with my thumb, I realized I hadn't thought past bringing her back to my hotel the night before. Now that I've had her in my bed, I knew I needed more of her. If she had stayed I would have taken her out to breakfast. Kept her until lunch. I would have wanted her to stay the weekend. I needed more of her.

Shaking my head, I refocused on the empty hotel room. I needed to pack up.

Fifteen minutes later I was settled in an identical room across the hotel. My phone rang, and I saw the name of my new coworker who had dragged me out the night before. "Hey, Cooper. What's up."

"Okay, Mr. Deir. So I told my dad you didn't have any family."

"I have family, Cooper. And I already told you to call me Fitz..."

"No, can do, boss. Dad said you have to come over for dinner tonight. My aunts are totally nuts and will try to hook you up with my cousins, but don't do it. Trust me, my cousin

Nova seems pretty at first, but she is nuts, she just broke up with her boyfriend and she is on the prowl. Aside from that, it should be good grub."

Looking around my empty room, I didn't see any reason not to take Cooper up on his offer. Lina hadn't mentioned what she was doing, and I didn't even get her number before she took off with no notice. Granted, I was a heavy sleeper. We made no promises that night. It could have been a one-time thing. But I felt something. I was sure she did, too. Maybe I was wrong if she left without even waking me up.

"Okay, I'll see you around noon. Text me the address."

As I was about to get into my car, I stopped by the front desk where Walter was standing behind the counter.

"Hi, Walter. Could I leave a note, I'm expecting a friend to stop by and I want her to know I moved rooms."

Walter nodded at me, handing me a pad of yellowing hotel stationery. "You could always use those new-fangled machines you kids keep in your pocket too, you know."

Chagrined, I didn't have the heart to tell him I didn't know her number.

"Covering all my bases." I finished writing my information down and folded it into a square.

I watched as Walter placed the note in an envelope.

"What's the name again?" the old man asked.

"Lina."

"Ah, maybe I know her." He nodded pleasantly. "Lived here in Little Norway all my life, I know just about everyone. I might know this Regina."

"Somehow I believe you." I chuckled. He didn't seem like the type to sleep with a woman and not know her number, or where she worked, or her full name. I wasn't about to admit that to the man. "And it's Lina."

Walter waved at me as he taped the note to the desk.

TOO EARLY IN THE GAME

Lina

With the liquid courage of two mimosas, I talked my younger cousin, Jason, into giving me a ride down to the Ridgewood Inn and Suites. I was crazy to think that he would want to come over, but he had mentioned his mom was out of town. The idea of Fitz sitting all alone in that little room for Thanksgiving made me sad. I could at least offer, right? If the whole thing was a one-night and never to be seen again situation, then he could say no. While Jason sat in the car, I walked up to room 209, knocking three times. There was silence behind the door. I knocked again, a sense of disappointment settling over me. Until that moment, I didn't want to admit how much I was hoping to see Fitz again. To say that night had been the most incredible night of my life was an understatement. Not only was the sex incredible, but he seemed to get me on a level I had never experienced before. Without talking, and admittedly, once we started kissing, there was almost no talking. We connected on a level I didn't know was possible.

While I understood that sometimes a one-night stand is just that, I realized I wanted more with Fitz. And I wanted to believe he wanted more from me. Why hadn't I left my number? What kind of bonehead doesn't leave a number?

The kind who doesn't have one-night stands.

Every other guy I had slept with, I had known for months, sometimes years, before we slept together. I knew their phone numbers; I knew where they lived and their mother's maiden names.

I didn't even know Fitz's last name. Or where he worked. Down on the second level, my cousin honked his horn, hanging out the window. "Are you bringing your booty call to dinner or not?"

I leaned over the balcony and flipped him off. "He's not here. I'm going to leave a note at the front desk for him."

Walking to the empty front desk, I hit the small bell on the counter. A girl I went to junior high with walked out, her eyes flicking distastefully down my body before raising a brow.

"Hey, Sandy." I said, more cheerful than I meant to sound. "How's, um..." Wracking my brain for the name of the boyfriend Sandy had years before. "Rick?"

Her face implacable, Sandy stared me down. "How should I know?"

I always was rubbish at small talk. "I was going to leave a note for the guy staying in 209. Fitz..."

"There is no one in 209." Sandy interrupted as if bored with me already.

"Yes, there is, I was just there a few hours ago."

"The gentleman in 209 checked out an hour ago."

"Well, do you have any contact information for him?"

"I will not disclose that information to you. I could lose my job."

"Not even his last name?" I asked.

Sandy raised a brow, looking me up and down with a sneer. "You don't even know his last name?"

I felt the pink heat of my cheeks. "Um, well, it was a bit crazy last night, and he said he was staying here until the 1st, so I thought..."

Smacking her gum, Sandy's eyes went back to the computer screen, somehow more bored than moments before. "Well, he checked out of 209. Can't help you. Sorry." Sandy turned away, walking to the back room.

Sandy was definitely not sorry. Grumbling, I walked back to the waiting car. Sandy was probably still pissed about the time that I got to be Veruca Salt in our eighth-grade rendition of Charlie and Chocolate Factory. Sandy got cast as one of the bedridden grandmas. Climbing in beside Jason, I shook my head.

"Bummer," my cousin said, before flipping the car into reverse.

Back at my parent's house and an enormous glass of Malbec later, I opened my laptop, ready to do some light internet stalking of Fitz. Google, okay. First name... Fitz. That had to be a nickname. What could that be short for, Fitzrandolph? Fitzwilliam? Oh, Fitzwilliam might be cool. Like Darcy from Pride and Prejudice. Why hadn't I asked him that? Did I know anything about the man?

Focus, Lina. Focus.

Okay, Fitz, short for something, just moved to the area for work. He didn't like rhubarb beer?

No, that's you that doesn't like rhubarb beer.

I checked Facebook, but there was no Fitz to be found. An indie pop band, ads for a furniture company and various people with last names that started with Fitz. But no one in the area with Fitz as a first name or a last name. No mutual friends, no posts in the Ridgewood community page about speed bumps or Randall, the peacock that wandered the highway. No Fitz anywhere.

Frustrated, I clicked over to my work email to see what Black Friday sales were going to bankrupt me this year. An unread email sat between a reminder not to park in assigned parking spots at the college and a sales advert for a vegan makeup brand.

To: emcconnell@ridgewoodcc.edu
From: jfdier@pmhs.org
Subject: Your Adoption application #30751

Mr. William McConnell,

I hope this email finds you well. Thank you for your interest in adopting Otis from Port Madison Humane Society. Attached you will find your online application you completed on November 19th. Please review the information to ensure everything is correct and fill out the questionnaire. Once you have completed the application and questionnaire, it will be reviewed by our adoption team to ensure that Otis will placed in the correct home. Here at Port Madison Humane Society, the safety and well being of our animals is our first priority.

As mentioned in the paperwork, Otis requires a special diet and will be on medication for the rest of his life. He requires an owner who is prepared to take care of his specific needs.

Respectfully,
Jeremiah F. Deir

Adoption Coordination Director
Port Madison Humane Society

Confused, I reread the email a few times, then because I was nosy, read the attached application where a middle-aged man in a nearby town was looking for a dog. I typed *Port Madison Humane Society* into the search engine and found their website matched the email address. So, it wasn't a scam and instead was a simple typing error. I looked up the picture of the aforementioned Otis. The picture was of a very large tan dog with a dark brown face and a big lolling tongue. I shot back a quick response to the Humane Society.

To: jfdier@pmhs.org
From: emcconnell@ridgewoodcc.edu
Subject: Re: Your Adoption application #30751

Mr. Deir,

Hi, as cute as Otis is, (I looked him up on the website), I am not Mr. McConnell and cannot adopt him. I looked through the application, and as I am not a 57-year-old who lives in a five-bedroom home with a fenced backyard in Manzanita, I don't think it will work out.

I am a 24-year-old preschool teacher at the child development center at Ridgewood Community College (not that far from Manzanita!) who lives in an apartment. As much as I'd love a dog, I don't think an English Mastiff would be allowed or that my roommate would appreciate it.

If I could be so bold, I think you might have hit E
instead of W when writing the email address. I hope
you can get a hold of Mr. McConnell. (If my memory
of the staff directory is right, I think he teaches
calculus.)

E. (Not W.) McConnell

After emailing, I snapped my laptop shut. Beside me, the family dog, Roscoe, nudged my hand. Burying my fingers in his thick caramel fur, I scratched behind his ears. His pink tongue lolled out, much like Otis from the email. I wished I could have a dog in my apartment, but knew that between mine and Zoya's stuff, there was barely room for a goldfish, let alone a 150-pound dog.

In a few months, Zoya would move out when she and her boyfriend from high school, Milo Bellamy, would get married. Zoya's parents were very traditional and forbade her from living with her fiance before marriage. Zoya agreed to live with me only because then she could have Milo over whenever she wanted and have time to plan the wedding.

But all that would change soon. For the first time, I'd be living on my own. With my job at the center, I could barely afford my portion of the rent. Preschool teachers were woefully underpaid, and my job was no exception. I would either have to move back in with my parents in June or find another roommate. Neither sounded like a fun idea.

Resting my chin on my hand, I could feel a tender spot on my jaw where Fitz's stubble had scratched me. Fingering the abrasion, a pulse of heat drove through me, remembering his kiss on my skin, the feel of his hands on my hips, the heat of

his breath against my ear. I had never experienced a night like
that before. I was ruined.

COUPLES WE KNOW

Fitz

Back at my desk after the weekend, I turned my computer on to sort through the adoption applications that came in over the weekend. Thanksgiving weekend was always a big one, with families deciding they needed a new pet for the holidays. Between the application for a family of five looking to adopt a rabbit was a response for the placement application for Otis. I scanned the contents and groaned. While it wasn't the worst thing that could have happened, the application included some private information. I didn't think I would get fired over that, but it wasn't an impossibility. Reading the person's response, I chuckled. At least they had a good sense of humor about it. I shot the person a quick email back and then re-sent the email the correct recipient who was indeed a calculus teacher at the same college this E. McConnell seemed to work at.

To: emcconnell@ridgewoodcc.edu
From: jfdier@pmhs.org
Subject: re: re: Your Adoption application #30751

E. (Not W.),

Thank you for getting back to me. I might have waited around for a while for Mr. McConnell's application.

You are absolutely right. I did type E instead of W. I think the rush of getting everything done before Thanksgiving has me distracted. It's my first month on the job, and I'm embarrassed that I made such a big mistake. Thank you for letting me know.

Since you have already seen our website, we have several animals here that would be a good fit for a 24-year-old preschool teacher, especially one who is responsible enough to respond to a mistaken email. Maybe a kitten? I've attached a few photos of some kittens we will put up for adoption in the next few days. If you ask me, Retta-Mae is pretty cute. You can thank me for the sneak peek when you come in to fill out an adoption application.

Respectfully,
Jeremiah F. Deir
Adoption Coordination Director
Port Madison Humane Society

I moved on to the long list of applications I had on my desk. Some people thought they could just come into a shelter and pick out the pet they wanted with no questions. The process was far more involved than that. Most of the time, people had to answer a list of questions correctly before they could even see the animals. What is their home like? Do they have children and if so what are the ages? How often are they away from home?

Francine Crosby, the shelter's veterinarian popped her head into the room.

"Parsley has passed the checkup and should be ready for adoption by Monday." Francine was pulling the sleeves down on her red and green flannel.

I glanced up to grin at the older woman. "I was wondering how my favorite little lady was doing."

The cat had come in a week before; dropped off at our surrender station in the middle of the night. The orange and white cat had seemed to be on death's door when Cooper had found her that morning, but with a healthy diet of wet food and medicine, she was making a fast recovery.

"She's doing good, she'll get adopted out in no time, I just know it."

"Good, good," I looked from Francine back to my screen. Only a few weeks into the position, I already knew if you engaged Francine in conversation, she could talk for hours. The near miss with Otis's paperwork had me on edge. I couldn't have any more delays in getting my work done.

Instead of taking the hint, the veterinarian walked further into the room. "Speaking of little ladies, I don't see a ring on that finger." She glanced at my barren desk. "Do you have someone special in your life?"

Joining the staff of a shelter in the small town came with a high level of curiosity and a low level of personal boundaries. I could already tell that living in Ridgewood was going to open me up to this line of questioning. "Are you asking me out, Dr. Crosby?"

The woman threw her head back to laugh, a bawdy sound that matched her clean face and crinkled the lines around her gray eyes. Straightening, she patted her short silver hair, her cheeks pink. "If I had met you thirty years ago, absolutely, but no, my daughter. Imogen. She just graduated from Southeastern and is moving back to town. She's twenty-four, has a degree in communications, and was hired to be the event planner for the city. And she loves cats and Thai food."

"She sounds lovely, Dr. Crosby..."

"She is lovely. Looks just like me thirty years ago." Straightening, she preened in front of me. "I may not look like it now, but I was a looker in my days. I'll give you Imogen's number. You'll call her for coffee."

I gave her a smile. "As wonderful as your daughter sounds, I'm afraid, I'm a little busy getting settled into town to be looking to date."

Dr. Crosby eyed me, frowning. "It's just coffee, Jeremiah."

"You can call me Fitz, Dr. Crosby." It seemed that before I started the director had told everyone of my coming and now I was having to break them of the habit of calling me by my first name. Leaning back in my chair I studied the veterinarian. "Does your daughter know you're setting her up on dates?"

Dr. Crosby flapped her hand as if dismissing the comment. "She has terrible taste in men. All I'm doing nudging her in the right direction."

I declined to mention that her daughter would likely be embarrassed to find her mother setting her up with men she barely knew as well as telling them about her dating misdeeds. "Dr. Crosby. I am flattered but now isn't a good time. Check back in a few months to see if your meddling will work then."

The doctor didn't seem to be offended by the comment. "I'm holding you to that."

Glancing back at my desktop I saw an email waiting from E. McConnell.

     To: jfdier@pmhs.org
     From: emcconnell@ridgewoodcc.edu
     Subject: Cute pictures

No thank you needed. Just doing my good deed for the day. I know how annoyed I'd be if I was waiting for an email that never came.

And, okay, yes, I admit Retta-Mae is very cute. I do want to get a pet soon. My parents kept my yellow lab when I went off to college and while he is still alive and well at my parents' house and they only live a few minutes down the road from me, it's not the same as having one in my home. Over time, my beloved Roscoe turned traitor and now sleeps in my brother's room. Maybe it's time for me to cut my losses and accept that I will have to fill the Roscoe shaped hole in my life with a new pet. I'll think about your kitten proposition.

Smiling to myself, I moved on to the next item on my to-do list, but not before setting a notification if I got another email from this E. McConnell.

JUST THE SAME
Lina

Before I could get out of my car, my father was jogging down the driveway. "Evie, drive me to the store." A glance at the five cars parked around my dad's truck showed me all I needed to know. My mother had instructed me to come over to make Christmas cookies. With that came my mother's two sisters. And their kids, and Aunt Cathy's Pomeranian, Sukie.

"Does this call for wine or beer?" I got back in the driver's seat as my father waited outside the car for me to clear off the debris on the passenger seat. I kept a tidy classroom, but my car was always a step away from a hazmat area. After throwing three travel cups and a Halloween scarf in my backseat, I waved him in.

"Bourbon." He sat down, then arched his back, grabbing a wad of plastic gloves and clean tissues I normally kept in my coat pocket for playground emergencies. Snagging it out of his hand, I tossed it into the backseat. My dad shook his head at me. "You need to clean out this car. You're going to get rats."

I turned the car on and glanced over my shoulder to pull back out on the road. "Don't be ridiculous Dad. It's not that bad."

"I think I saw a cockroach scuttling around in here."

"Most of this stuff is papers from school. Library books, fabric for the classroom. There are only a few crumbs."

"Boys like a clean space, you know."

"If a guy is grossed out by clean tissues and a twenty-four pack of glitter, then he's not the right kind of guy for me."

My dad started pushing buttons on my dashboard, grumbling about how he didn't understand touch screens in cars.

I brushed his hand away and set the radio to the sports station so he could listen to the Kraken's game. I suspected before I pulled up he was hiding in the garage with his portable radio with its coat hanger antennae.

"Whatever happened to that one guy, Timmy?"

I leaned forward to see around a large hedge before pulling out on the main road. "Who?"

"You know, that one boyfriend of yours."

"Mickey? Do you mean Mickey? My boyfriend from junior high?" I pulled into the store parking lot. "Dad, I have no idea what happened to him. I literally haven't seen the guy for seven years."

My dad shrugged. "I liked him. Remember when he vacuumed our stairs?" My father's eyes got misty and he sighed dramatically. "That was a good boyfriend."

I refrained from telling my father that the guy was kicked out of school after continually showing up drunk and was now likely in prison. "Come on, let's get your provisions."

The scent of sugar and strawberry hit me as I walked in the front door. Once we returned from the store, my father walked straight into the garage, no doubt to resume the radio sports until the extended family left. Left to fend for myself, I hugged the empty Tupperware to my chest. In a few hours my mother would insist on filling it before I left.

Sukie yipped at my ankles as I walked around the noisy black and brown puff, careful not to step on her paw. From the corner, Roscoe lifted his golden brown head and gave me a look of *I've had enough of that little dog.*

"Lina, you're finally here! You said noon!" Hands kneading a ball of dough, my mother shot me a disapproving look. "Your cousin Jason had to roll the Russian tea cakes and his balls are too small."

At the table, Jason looked up from his phone his mouth gaping in outrage. Suppressing a laugh, I walked over to press a kiss on my mother's cheek. "Sorry Mom. I got held up. I'm sure Jason's balls will be fine."

"Can everyone stop talking about my balls?" Jason grumbled. I gave him a mock salute and Jason flipped me off, narrowing his eyes at me.

My mother pointed me to the sink to wash up, reminding me to wash the back of my hands as well, as if I was still five. At the counter Aunt Cathy was beside Aunt Bea. My Yia-Yia liked alphabetic naming for her girls. Agnes; my mother, then Bernice, Catherine, and the perpetually late Dorothy. Aunt Dottie would show up in an hour when the cookies were almost done and help herself to the spoils.

Despite being adept at baking, when my mother and her sisters were in their mode, I was relegated to fetching ingredients and little else. Each year, the sisters baked cookies in the same order; thumbprints with jam, Russian tea cakes, chocolate peppermint crinkles, a basic sugar for decorating and caramel squares. I dug the cocoa powder and peppermint extract out of the back of the cupboard.

"Lina, you'll never guess who was asking about you at work?" Aunt Bea asked. Before I could answer Bea answered. "That nice boy, Matt Hanson. You know the one, his family owns the hardware store."

"Yes, I know Matt." I hedged.

"He said he saw you at the Skol House the other day. He said you looked like you're doing well." Bea wiggled her brows at me to emphasize her point.

As I set the ingredients down, I turned to her. "Theia, you know Matt Hanson just got divorced, right?"

"Well, first marriages don't always work out…" Bea nodded her head toward Cathy who was on her third husband.

"But do they normally end because he got his wife's best friend pregnant?"

"Relationships are complicated, you are in no position to judge others, Evangelina Grace." My mother interrupted.

I grabbed a hot cookie off the cooling rack and stuffed it in my mouth. My family meant well, but there was no way they could be serious about me dating Matt Hanson.

"Don't eat the good ones, if you're going to snack, eat the broken ones." My mother chided, swatting at my hand as I snagged a lopsided thumbprint and held it up for my mother's approval. She nodded with narrowed eyes.

"I'm not dating Matt Hanson." I shoved the crumbly goodness in my mouth.

"Of course you can't date him. All Bea was pointing out is there are single eligible men in this town. This is the time to meet someone. While you still have your youthful radiance."

"What does that even mean? Youthful radiance," I snorted, shoving another cookie in my mouth. Holiday treats were dangerous.

"It means your ass and tits haven't fallen down." My Aunt Dottie came through the door.

"For goodness sake, Dottie." My mother said.

Dottie ignored her older sister, pressing a kiss to the top of Jason's head then mine. Setting a bottle of wine in the middle table Dottie unwrapped the scarf around her neck, draping it over the back of a chair. Bea walked behind her, grabbing the scarf and hanging it on the coat rack, tutting while she moved.

"Alright, Kazan girls, what gossip have I missed?"

"Mom was trying to set Lina up with Matt Hanson," Jason said, his words garbled with cookies.

"That philander? No, our Lina can do better than that asshole."

"Dorothy!" Cathy admonished.

Jason snorted beside me. I shot him a warning glare.

On the floor in the dramatic play area, I held the plastic plate in my hand as two of my student's bustled around me cooking a wooden watermelon slice and a rubber steak in a baking pan. My eyes scanned the classroom as I was being served, doing a head count of the students. My co-teacher had left to take her break. While I was in ratio, when you're the only teacher in the room, you have to always be looking for situations to diffuse before they escalate. In the block area, a boy was building a tower almost as tall as himself and a girl was at the table gluing what had to be over fifty pompoms to paper. I made a mental note to be the one to get that piece of art off the table and not have the child do it, lest the glue and pompoms would fall off the paper and someone would cry. Likely her. Possibly. Sticky glue and oatmeal were the worst to get off the floor.

The door opened and in walked the uncle of one of my little chefs, Kylie. The same guy who stood me up the week of Thanksgiving.

"Uncle Chad!" Kylie yelled as she dumped the wooden watermelon and rubber steak on my lap. Chad picked up his niece, swinging her around. I set the fake food in its wicker basket before standing to walk over to the doorway.

When I approached, Chad set Kylie down. "Oh, hey, Lina."

"It's Ms. Lina, Uncle Chad."

"Right, Ms. Lina. How are you?"

I grabbed the sign in binder off the top of the cubbies. "I'm good. Kylie's dad didn't mention that you'd be picking up today."

"Oh, yeah, Tom got held up at work. He asked me to grab the little monster."

Pursing my lips, I groaned inwardly. This is why I should have never agreed to go out with the guy. I knew I'd be annoyed when I saw him again. "You'll need to sign her out here. First and last name and time."

As he was signing, he talked to me. "How have you been? I still want that rain check on the date."

I pretended I didn't hear him. "We were about to have an afternoon snack, so she's going to be hungry soon."

"Okay, I can feed her, now about that da..."

"She has a few coats in her cubby, you'll want to grab those." I bent down and gave Kylie a hug goodbye. "Have a good night Ky. We'll see you on Monday, okay?" Ignoring Chad, I turned away, settling myself at the table between the block builder and the pompom artist. Taking the glue bottle from the girl, I handed her a paintbrush and modeled how to spread the glue over the paper. My back to the door I waited until the door clicked shut.

A few minutes later my co-teacher, Juniper reappeared. "I saw Kylie's hot uncle was here."

Rolling my eyes, I shook my head. "He isn't that hot."

Juniper settled down next to the block builder. "If you say so." Turning to the little boy she smiled. "I think Kylie's uncle looks like a very nice man, don't you think, Cody?"

The little boy reached over his head to set the last block on the tower. I watched as the wooden structure shifted, leaning to one side before crashing to the floor. The boy began to cry and Juniper scooped him up in her arms. I turned back to the pompom artist, helping her slide the heavily glued paper onto a tray where it would need to dry for a week.

Juniper was right, Chad was an attractive man. He seemed like a good uncle to Kylie. I didn't know too much about him, but he was probably fine. He even had a good excuse for canceling their date weeks before. But after meeting Fitz, I had no interest in dating Chad, Diego Luna, or Alexander Calvert. Any hope of being attracted to another person was demolished.

I wasn't mad at Chad for canceling our date. He was the catalyst for the night. He was the symptom. It was easier to be mad at Chad than to admit how crazed I was feeling over not seeing Fitz. I was mad that I allowed myself to be so taken in by this man that I knew nothing about. That I was now stuck here, feeling foolishly moony over a complete stranger. Three orgasms was not love. So why did I feel so sick for him?

RINGING IN THE NEW

Fitz

After loading the last of my belongings into my car, the affectionately named "Boobaru", after the many dings and dents it withstood over the years, I stopped by the front desk. "Hey, I left a note up here for someone, Lina? I was wondering if you could tell me if she picked it up? It was a few days ago."

The young woman glanced up at me, her expression bored. "Lina? You said, Lina?"

"Yeah, Lina."

The women sigh loudly and shuffled things around the desk before holding up an envelope and scanning the front. "There's an envelope for a Regina."

I considered the envelope. It was possible the man had heard me wrong and wrote Regina. Or it could have been a different person all together. If Lina picked it up, then what did that mean? I would not be desperate for a girl who didn't want me. My self-worth was higher than that. Maybe. I thought back to how Lina asked me if I believed in signs. While I wasn't sure then, this felt like a big sign saying, *You're wasting your time, dude.*

"Thanks, um..." I glanced at her name tag. "Sandy."

"Sure thing Mr. Deir." She glanced away, looking back at the tablet in front of her, which seemed to be playing a popular true crime show.

Despite her not looking at me anymore, I nodded my good-bye and left, making my way to work. At lunch, I would get the keys to my new rental. The movers were meeting me there after work and I planned on a big night of unpacking, pizza and beer from the brewery next door. Just not the rhubarb.

To: emcconnell@ridgewoodcc.edu
From: jfdier@pmhs.org
Subject: re: cute pictures

Ms. McConnell,

I'm assuming you are a Ms. or a Mrs. Please correct I'm if I'm wrong, I hate to gender stereotype preschool teachers. I know the feeling of leaving a pet home. My cat, Hank, is living faithfully at my mother's home. I'm still adjusting to living in town, but once I've settled in, I'm going to get a pet. Good thing I have the first crack at the animals here. It's nice to be the adoption director sometimes. You sound like you've lived in the area for a while. Could you tell me where the best pizza is? I'm coming from Seattle, where there are a lot more options.

I'll tell Retta-Mae "Hi" for you.

Hungry,
Jeremiah F. Deir
Adoption Coordination Director
Port Madison County Humane Society

There, not too much. Just a friendly request for a food recommendation. Nothing nefarious in that. I certainly had a bunch of new coworkers I could ask for ideas on food, but this way, I could keep talking to this person.

I wasn't sure why I kept writing to this E. McConnell. Our exchange before had more than served its purpose. I responded politely and thanked her for her help. So why did I keep writing, then deleting an email to her? Or him. It could be a him. No, something told me it was a woman. I wasn't sure what the pull was, but I kept thinking back to Lina and the pull I had toward her. How when I saw her, I just knew talking to her would be worth it. I had never asked a woman from a bar to go home with me, and certainly not after only a few minutes. But something told me to ask her and it was the best night of my life. That same voice was telling me to write to this E. McConnell.

After three more applications, a tidying up of the small inventory in our pet supply store, and a small tussle with a Russian blue and a British Maine Coon that left me with a scratch on my hand, I was starving. Checking my email once again I saw E. McConnell's name and brightened.

To: jfdier@pmhs.org
From: emcconnell@ridgewoodcc.edu
Subject: Pizza Pie

J,

Yes, I am a Ms. It's not too far of a jump to gender stereotype my field. 97% of preschool teachers are women. It's actually something I would like to see change, but I digress.

As for pizza, I would recommend Flippy's down the street from the Humane Society, their stuffed crust pizza is pretty good. Now, personally, I think that if you are in Ridgewood and just want takeout; you need to get your pizza from Ridgewood Market. I know I can hear your skepticism from here. A grocery store? But I promise, it's worth it. They have great pizza. Just don't go in the middle of the day, that's when all the high school kids are down there. It's a zoo.

Of course, I'm assuming since you work with animals all day, you might like the zoo, but a gaggle of six-teen-year-old girls sitting at plastic tables can be a bit much for even the bravest of men. (I should know, I used to be one of those sixteen-year-olds.) Let me know what you think of the pizza.

:)

With a pizza box balanced on my hand, I let myself into my new place. Cooper and I went to lunch together and he insisted I bring home the leftovers.

Over pizza and jo-jos, Cooper had relegated me with all sorts of stories about the people who lived in Ridgewood. He knew everyone and our lunch was interrupted at least a dozen times by people young and old coming over to say hi to him. I lost count of how many times I had to wipe pizza off my hands with a napkin after Cooper introduced me.

True to E. McConnell's word, the pizza at Flippy's was good. They didn't have my favorite hot sauce there, but tabasco could work in an emergency. The entire lunchtime I was trying to ask him about Lina, but the phrasing was holding me back. Cooper knew everyone and seemed to love talking about everyone. As a new guy in town, I didn't want my business broadcast on Radio Ridgewood.

How could I tell him I met Lina on Thanksgiving and was still obsessing over her a week later without raising red flags? Cooper was a smart guy, he'd see right through me. Instead, I ate the potatoes and pizza as I plotted the best way to track Lina down.

Hours later and now home, I was no closer to finding out who she was. In a city of eleven thousand people, a beautiful dark-haired woman shouldn't be that hard to find. But all my efforts had been in vain. I went to the Skol House a few more times; I went to Ridgewood Market every day hoping I'd see her next to the Dungeness crab and live oyster tank, but no.

My new place was stuffed full of boxes on top of boxes. Christening my fridge with a six-pack of beer and the leftover pizza, I turned to survey the small home.

Less than eight hundred square feet the Easter egg-colored bungalow was wedged between two other pastel-painted homes in what I was told locals called "the skittle houses". Years before it had been the old military housing left to rot and had been inhabited by the lowest-income families. Now the houses were smushed together in neat rows with no cars allowed in the driveway and a maximum of two potted plants allowed on each porch.

This rental home was only a jumping-off point for me. If this job worked out, and I had hoped it would, I would find a bigger place later. Until then the two-bedroom place would fit nicely with me and my stuff.

I set to work, assembling my bed and making it. I'd need a place to sleep. In the bedroom's corner were my clothes packed up into boxes. I wasn't about to go through those. I could still live in my uniform of slacks and one of the Port Madison Humane Society shirts I had been given upon hire.

Heading to the kitchen I popped open a bottle of beer before opening the first box labeled "dishes and shit." Staring down at the mish-mash of a packing job I did when I left my last place, I cursed.

I really needed to be a better planner instead of working in the moment. Taking a swig, I realized that applied to too many things to count.

HORNS ALL BLOW

Fitz

I had no idea who this E. McConnell was, but I liked her. She didn't seem to take herself too seriously. She had good pizza recommendations and worked with kids. It was fun to talk to someone with no expectations. It helped to soothe the ache that thinking about Lina caused in my chest. I vowed I would figure out where she was. I would just have to be a little more creative in my detective skills.

To: emcconnell@ridgewoodcc.edu
From: jfdier@pmhs.org
Subject: teaser

Retta-Mae says Hi. Here is another picture in case you forgot what she looks like. She's a domestic shorthair, 11 weeks old. She's doing well at litter box training and loves playing with the feather teaser.

You were right about the pizza. The night I moved into my new place, I got some and it was surprisingly good. Especially paired with a variety pack of beer from Sticky Cow Brewery. I'm lucky enough I can walk there from my place. The pizza went well with the amber, but I'm not a fan of the dandelion beer. Who would want to drink a weed? That place is pretty adventurous.

Jeremiah F. Deir
Adoption Coordination Director
Port Madison County Humane Society

Only minutes later, I got a response. I smiled as I read through the email.

To: jfdier@pmhs.org
From: emcconnell@ridgewoodcc.edu
Subject: re: teaser

Okay, okay, I get it. Retta-Mae is adorable. You're starting to convince me. Now I just need to convince my roommate to take allergy pills so I can have a kitten.
Yeah, Sticky Cow has some bold choices in beer. It's not my type, but they have quite a few fans who love their takes on beer. Fun fact about that place. I planted the cedar tree that is in the back corner of the patio area. My parents know the original owners. I got the sapling in kindergarten for arbor day and planted it. Eighteen years later, there is my tree. Next time you're there enjoying an IPA, you can think of me and my exemplary pizza recommendations.

:)

Over the weekend, I started unpacking the boxes scattered around my new house. When I had downtime, I tried to find Lina. There was no trace of her on any of the normal social media. I found a Lina Hershey, who lived nearby in Illahee. I found Lina Park Bowling Lanes. But no Lina who lived in Ridgewood. The only person I was friends with on Facebook from Ridgewood was Cooper. It was possible I could have asked Cooper about Lina, but what would he say? Cooper seemed like a gossip, and I didn't think it was right to talk about my sex life to someone I was now supervising. I had professional standards, after all.

At night I went to the brewery. Only a few doors down from the Skol House where we met, I hoped to catch a glimpse of Lina or even her friend. I became friendly with the brewmaster and had lengthy conversations about hops and malt. I sat beside the outdoor fire pit. For the first time in days, the typical drizzle had relented. Weather in the Pacific Northwest wasn't as much torrential downpour but nine months of incessant mist a few degrees above freezing. December was always the rainiest of the months. The weather report was calling for snow in the next week, but I doubted that. Forecasts about snow almost always were exaggerated and when they did occur rarely lasted more than a week. Pulling my fleece jacket tighter around myself, I leaned back in the Adirondack chair. From my spot by the fire, I could see over the high-pitch roofs of Front Street and into the sailboat-lined marina of Freedom Bay. While I had lived in various cities in Western Washington, I had never had the chance to settle into a place that so casually had beautiful views and this hometown feel. Sure, the nearest department store was over thirty minutes away, and there was only one option for Indian food in town, but that was okay with me. The town boasted more than enough breweries and had a surprisingly large number of expensive art galleries. I was enjoying the Nordic kitsch the town boasted. The little gnomes painted on store windows, the large Viking statue with its sign *Velkommen til*

Ridgewood that Dr. Crosby told me was decorated differently for each holiday. It currently wore a Santa hat and sting of bulb lights around its neck. I liked the window display at Sluy's Bakery with its selection of lefse and krigla cookies alongside gingerbread house kits.

Beer in hand, I rested my feet against the side of the fire pit, a construction of chicken wire, cinder blocks, and oyster shells. Inside my pocket, my phone buzzed and as I pulled it out I groaned. I was supposed to call my mother when I got off work earlier, but once I got home and the full boxes overwhelmed me it slipped my mind.

"Hi, Ma."

"Don't you, *Hi Ma,* me, Jeremiah Fitzgerald, you were supposed to call me hours ago." I heard the running of water and dishes knocking together. She must have called me on speakerphone, her voice was far away.

"Yeah, sorry about that. It was a long day. I'm just getting in. How are you doing, Ma? Sound like you're cleaning up from dinner?"

The water turned off and her voice became clearer. "Alvita was over. I made her one of those pot pies from the store."

"I'm sure she had something to say about that." My mother's best friend, Alvita, had big opinions about ready-made food from the shop. As successful as my mother was, cooking homemade dinners fell down the list of her priorities.

"You know I didn't call you to talk about Costco."

"I didn't think so, but you--"

She cut me off. "I'm making sure you're still coming over for Christmas."

I took a long swallow of my Valhalla IPA before answering. "Of course I am. Why wouldn't I?"

"Well, Ridgewood is so far. I wasn't sure if you could make the long trek. I haven't seen you in almost a month—I go days without hearing from you. Don't know if you're alive or dead."

"Ma, I've been busy getting settled. I've been unpacking my stuff at the house. Getting a feel for the job. And Ridgewood is only an hour away on the ferry. An hour and a half if I drive around. You're acting like I'm across the country instead of across Puget Sound."

"Could have fooled me." My mother sniffed on the other end.

"Ma," I warned. "The ferry goes both ways. Besides, this time of year, I know you're swamped with grading before the break."

She gave me a noncommittal sound that let me know I was right, but she would never admit it.

"Are you bringing anyone with you? You still talking to that one girl, Helga?"

I fought the urge to roll my eyes. Even from thirty miles as a crow flies away, she would somehow know. "Harley, Ma. We dated for six months, I brought her to the house a few times. But no. I haven't talked to her in over a year. She lives in Denver now. Pretty sure she has a new boyfriend."

There was a moment of silence where I could tell my voice was too sharp with my mother. "You didn't answer my question."

I thought of Lina. If I could have, I would have invited her. Only a few hours together but the idea of her going with me on Christmas played through my mind. The feel of her hand in mine as we drove in the car. Seeing her looking over the bow of the ferry as we crossed the water, the Space Needle and great wheel in front of her.

"And what question was that?" I asked before taking another sip of the hoppy beer.

"Are you bringing anyone with you for Christmas?"

"Ma, if I was serious enough about someone to bring them to Christmas, don't you think I'd tell you about her?"

On the other end, my mother sniffed, "I would like to think so, but I never know about you. First, you leave right before Christmas to start this new job and I don't know what you're eating or what kind of place you're living out of, I don't know your neighbors, and..."

"Ma." I sighed. When my father passed, it was me and her for years. Even when I left to go to school, she was a part of my decision. While I had been away for long periods from her, she always knew what I was doing before I made that choice. Except for this move and job. When I got the call that I was selected for this position, I was elated. I had worked for years at building my resume to run an animal rescue center. I couldn't pass up the opportunity, so I accepted the position and then broke the news to her. She never tried to stop me or tell me not to do something, but she worried. "Ridgewood is wonderful, you'll love it. I'll take you around and you'll want to buy a place here when I'm done giving you a tour."

"Well, I don't know about that." She said her tone slightly softer. "Now tell me more about your work."

I settled back into the chair, relaxing as I relayed some stories from my last few weeks on the job.

Halfway through a story about a temperamental chinchilla, my mother stopped me. "Shoot, that's the door. I got to go baby, but you call soon, okay? And next time, don't you roll your eyes at me, son. Don't think I didn't catch that," she chided.

I groaned. How does my mother always know?

"Love you, Ma. I'll see you in a few weeks, okay? I'll check in on Sunday, alright?"

Draining my glass, I wedged it between my thighs and stuck my hands in my pockets. The heat lamps and fire took little from the biting winter air. Inside the brewery crowds of people were trickling in and a band was setting up in the corner. I knew I should probably get in from the cold, but I couldn't yet. Gazing around the empty courtyard I saw the tree in the corner, the flat green cedar boughs sweeping the top of the white canvas tent. That was E's tree.

The night was muted shades of violet and black, the clear sky above me. Tipping my head back I gazed at the stars. As a child, my father would take me out in the backyard and show me the different constellations. The grass slightly wet on our backs. His slightly crooked finger pointed at the endless space above us. With my own crooked pointer finger I traced the line of Ursa Minor. The little bear.

I wondered what my father would say to the man I was today. Losing a parent at sixteen is a special sorrow. I was just coming into myself and now he would never see the man I had become.

I hoped I could make him proud.

THOUSAND INVITATIONS

Lina

S ettling into the snug leather armchair in the corner of Norse Brew, I took a drink of my holiday drink. I tried not to overindulge in such sugary drinks, but between feeling low about Fitz and the soggy state of December in the Pacific Northwest, I needed a pick me up. Outside my window, the town was preparing for its annual Julefest featuring a Lucia Bride and a bonfire in the big pit on the waterfront.

The one bright spot in my week was emailing the mysterious Jeremiah Dier. We had been emailing back and forth several times. I told him about how I lived my whole life in Ridgewood and used to want to go to attend Columbia University in New York, but instead settled for getting my degree from the same college I was currently working for. He told me about how he moved around a bunch as a child until his mother got tenure as an English professor. He mentioned his father passing when he was in his teens and how he and his mother leaned on one another through that. I told him about how stifling it could be to still live in the town you grew up in. How I've never lived further than ten minutes away from my parent's home and I see the same people every weekend. Sometimes, I run into my third-grade teacher in the shampoo aisle at the grocery store and a few weeks ago even had my shop teacher from junior high offer me a hit off his joint. I shared with him that while I didn't want to live anywhere else,

I still felt like the whole town had an idea of what kind of person I was without truly knowing me. Our conversations were getting increasingly intimate.

It wasn't all serious talk, though. He told me how he loved animals, snowboarding, and soccer. I told him about my love for teaching and reading historical romances. His favorite color is green. Mine is royal blue. He hates those little plastic price tags that stores put on clothes. And I hate the unofficial Pacific Northwest uniform of sandals and socks.

Setting my drink down, I thumbed to my spot in my favorite author's newest holiday romance. Losing myself in the set of enemies who found themselves at an inn on Christmas Eve with *only one bed* and the lingering looks over mutton pie and ale in the back room of the inn were getting intense. A shadow cast over my head and I ignored it. Viscount Rodolphe had just removed Lady Beatrice's glove and was about to touch her wrist. It was getting spicy in here.

A throat cleared above me, and I looked from the page to find Chad standing over me.

"Good book?" Chad scratched his head under his baseball hat emblazoned with the name of an indie rock band.

Setting my thumb inside the book to mark my spot I lowered it to my lap. "Yeah."

He glanced at the cover. A tanned, shirtless man about to kiss a woman in a red satin dress that was falling off her shoulders. "Looks very... cerebral."

Shoving the cardboard coffee sleeve between the pages, I put the book down on the table. "How many books do you read a year?"

He seemed to take the comment for an invitation. He settled into the leather chair beside me, his khakis showed signs of being hemmed over his stark white shoes. How he managed to not get those dirty in the perpetually grimy streets was a mystery. He probably cleaned them with a special toothbrush. I had nothing against a man who had high standards for cleanliness; it was better than the alternative, but something about his pristine white shoes rankled me. The night I met Fitz, he had slightly scuffed boots on, clean but obviously worn for function.

Beside me Chad spread his knees wide, his leg bumping against mine as he took up space in the small corner I held. I angled my legs away.

"Five to ten, I'd say. Mostly nonfiction. The last book I read was postmodern structuralism. It was a fascinating look at Cultural Materialism and I think..."

Realizing that he wasn't going to leave me alone, I interrupted him. "I read about a book a week. While this book isn't for nihilists who like to think themselves into holes, there's no reason to be derisive about my choice in reading. I don't belittle your choice to spend your days at a driving range."

"I don't... That is to say..." Chad wiggled his shoulder as if he could shake off the direction the conversation was going. Keeping my face blank I watched as he squirmed. Rubbing a hand over the back of his neck he had the decency to look chagrined. "I was just making a joke."

Leaning forward, I lowered her voice, "I sincerely hope that you have a better sense of humor than to make fun of a book that is a heavily researched look at class differences and gender inequity, all while having a compelling plot, is sex-positive and has complex representations of female characters."

His already pink cheeks managed a darker shade at my words. "I'm sorry. I didn't mean anything by my comments. When I saw you sitting over here and after our quick conversation when I was picking up Kylie, I wanted to talk to you again."

Softening, I sat back in my chair. Just because Fitz had ghosted me didn't mean that all guys were garbage. "Sorry, I'm a little grumpy. I like your hat." I motioned to his head. "Their song, Consecrated Beds is one of my favorites."

Chad pulled his hat off his head, to look at the front. His blonde hair was smashed against his skull in the front. "Oh, yeah, these guys are great."

Narrowing my eyes, I paused. "You know it's an all-girl band, right?"

Zoya and I had seen them a year before at the Showbox Sodo. While the lead singer had an androgynous voice, she was female-identifying and named Lacy. They were nominated best new artist at the Grammy's a few years before.

Chad coughed, "Uh, yeah, totally, I meant guys the way I call everyone dude. Gender neutral, of course."

I nodded along, though I doubted him. He's likely never wearing that hat again. "Sure, okay."

The barista called out an order for a black drip. Chad stood to get the coffee. Why would he order a drip at a coffee shop? You can make drip at home. Coffee shops are for drinks you can't make yourself. I brought my book back up to my face. Viscount Rodolphe was now inspecting a small birthmark on Lady Beatrice's wrist with a single finger.

The leather chair beside mine made a low farting noise as Chad sat back down. I considered ignoring him. A woman reading a romance novel in public should be enough of a fuck-off sign, but this man didn't take a hint.

Loudly slurping his coffee he watched me as I read. I had to reread the line about Viscount Rodolphe saying her smile was like the waxing moon, growing in light each day. Normally I'd get a little heart swoon after a soapy line like that but with Chad staring at me it fell flat.

Setting the book down on my lap I looked over at him. "Look, Chad. You seem like a nice guy, but I'm not interested in dating right now."

"Was it because I canceled? Because, I really had a work emergency. It wasn't some bullshit excuse."

I shook my head. "No, nothing like that. I'm just not feeling it." There wasn't a way I could tell him that no matter how good a guy he was, there was no interest for me when I had the most passionate night of my life with a stranger only weeks before. I didn't have to go out with Chad to know there was no spark between us. Even his shoes annoyed me.

"Are you seeing someone else? I don't get it, I have a lot going for me, Lina. I have a good job, make stacks, have good hair. I can deadlift two twenty. Plenty of chicks want me."

My teeth scraped against my lower lip as I tried not to laugh. Did he think that was impressive? Pink was creeping up his neck as he stared me down.

"Your loss, like I said, I can get other girls, hotter girls. You have no idea what you're missing."

"Okay," I agreed. Bringing my book back up to my face I reread the first sentence. Out of the corner of my eye, I saw Chad glaring at me before getting up with a huff, his drip coffee gripped so tight in his hand I thought it might burst.

Chad stomped away, shouldering the door open forcefully. Once he was on the other side of the door, I opened the book back up, scanning the lines until I found where I left off. The fire inside their room was burning low and I could tell they were about to kiss, but I couldn't get into it anymore. Sour mood, I set the book down and tilted my head back.

I couldn't spare a moment of regret for letting Chad down. In all honesty, I should have been rude. He wasn't the man for me. *I lift two-twenty*. Geez, I didn't know or care to know about weightlifting. If he thought I was that kind of woman we were not a good fit.

Why was dating so hard? They all said they wanted a nice girl, but what they meant was a meek girl. An accessory not an autonomous person with her own interests and life. This wasn't about Chad and his egotistical rant. It was every man I had met before him; it was the dumb chin nod Matt Hanson gave me and the way my last ex-boyfriend kept correcting my pronunciation of words in front of others.

While I should have known better, I thought what I had with Fitz was different. Special, even. But I must have been wrong about him too.

WELCOMING IN
Fitz

The application in my hand, my eyes glazed over from scanning the same line over and again. What I wanted to do was email E back. Our correspondence was becoming increasingly intimate. I had no idea who this girl was, but it was a distraction from thinking of Lina every other moment. There was a knock on my doorway. Glancing up I saw Dr. Crosby with a younger woman beside her. The woman had the same hazel eyes and scattering of freckles across her nose that Dr. Crosby had. I suspected the woman's shoulder-length caramel hair was the same color Dr. Crosby's was ten years before.

"Fitz. I'm so glad to see you in your office."

"That I am, Dr. Crosby. This must be the daughter you've told me so much about." Standing, I extended my hand. "I'm Fitz Deir."

The woman stepped forward. "Hi, Imogen. Ginny."

Dr. Crosby looked between us a glimmer in her eye. "Imogen just took me to lunch. She is a very dutiful daughter, I'm so lucky to have her."

"Mom," Ginny groaned under her breath.

Dr. Crosby clapped her hands together, "Oh, I forgot to give Paprika his second dose of the worms medicine. Fitz can keep you company. I'll be back in a jiffy."

Leaving them alone, Ginny gave me a small smile that seemed to say, *sorry about that.* We were silent for a few arduous moments before Ginny looked at me. "You know this was a ruse, right?"

Shoving my hands into the pockets of my slacks, I leaned back on my heels. "Yeah, your mother is a wonderful veterinarian, but she is a terrible liar."

"That she is. She insisted on me coming into the shelter when I dropped her off, saying she needed to give me something off her desk. Once we got in, she walked me straight here. She really is just looking out for me, but she can be a little..."

"My mother can be the same way, I know the feeling."

"I told her already, I have no interest in being set up. I'm just getting started at work and I don't have time to get distracted." She paused as her words sunk in. Her eyes widened, "No offense to you. You seem real... swell."

I fought the urge to laugh at the odd wording.

"No offense taken. I'm in the same position. In the five minutes I've known you, you also seem swell. And now we've established the other's niceness, I really should get back to work." Sticking out her hand, I shook it. There was no zing of appreciation for this attractive and single woman in front of me. It was a warm palm attached to an arm. I liked this Ginny Crosby, but there was no attraction. Dropping her hand, I shoved my hands back in my pockets. I couldn't help but compare the handshake to the first time I touched Lina. The recognition at the graze of skin against skin.

"Same."

A shadow outside the door shifted. In the window's reflection on the door, I could see Dr. Crosby listening in. "How's Paprika doing Dr. Crosby?" I called out.

Dr. Crosby stepped out, her face woefully guilty looking. "Paprika is fine. Doing well. A lovely cuddle bug."

"I should hope so, since Paprika was adopted yesterday." I kept my face devoid of emotion, but Ginny beside me burst into laughter.

"Okay, Mom. I love you bunches. I have to get back to work." She leaned forward and pressed a kiss to her mother's pink cheeks. Giving me a wave, she headed out the door. "Fitz, it was wonderful meeting you. You are indeed a *swell* person."

Once her daughter left, Dr. Crosby narrowed her eyes. "Maybe I don't want you dating my daughter if you're going to be so shifty."

Turning on her heels she left the office, as I called after her, "I shall persevere."

Shuffling the adoption form to the side I pulled up an update on how one of our pit bulls was doing in his foster home. Pits were notoriously hard to place because of poor public perception. Luckily we had a good network of volunteers and foster homes in the community.

Scanning my event calendar I set a reminder to repost the flyer for our upcoming Empty the Shelter event lasting through the end of the week. Our goal was the have most of the animals adopted out before the holiday. We had a good turnout, with many animals adopted, including Retta-Mae.

While I knew this E wouldn't adopt her, it was a good reason to email. Despite not being interested in Ginny Crosby, I was pulled toward this E. McConnell. I wondered what her name was. Elizabeth? Maybe Eden or Erin? I wondered what she looked like. If she had someone to eat pizza with. Before I could second guess myself, I wrote out the email, sending it to her and changing the playful dynamic to something more.

To: emcconnell@ridgewodcc.edu
From: jfdier@gchs.org
Subject: Bad News

Hi E,

I have bad news. Retta-Mae has been adopted. I know you had your heart set on her, but unfortunately she will live in luxury and only eat wet cat food for the rest of her life. We have a few more kittens left. If one sticks out to you, let me know and I can get you the application. Maybe a gift for your boyfriend?

Jeremiah F. Deir
Adoption Coordination Director
Port Madison County Humane Society

CRAZY TO SUPPOSE

Lina

I stared at the screen. Was this guy asking if I had a boyfriend? He was. I had no idea what he looked like, but man, was I curious. He couldn't have a girlfriend, could he? Guys don't ask that unless they're unattached. And I knew he was close to my age. Unless he graduated late in life. Before I could chicken out, I emailed back.

To: jfdier@pmhs.org
From: emcconnell@ridgewoodcc.edu
Subject: re: Bad News

I don't have a boyfriend. To be honest, I met a guy recently. I really liked him, but I guess the universe had different ideas of what's best for me. It didn't work out. I was excited when I met him, but he obviously wasn't as into me as I was into him. He ghosted me. I don't have a ton of dating experience, so maybe that's how it goes. I might have read the cues all wrong.

It's been a while since I've seen anyone. The last guy I seriously dated was less than trustworthy, if you catch my drift. He wanted to work things out, but if there is one thing I can't stand, it's someone who lies to me.

Wow, that got serious fast. I'm sad about Retta-Mae, but just as with my dating life, there are other kittens in the shelter. I suppose I'll have to move on from my hopes of Retta-Mae.

After emailing, I worried I had said too much. Admitting the last boyfriend I had cheated on me wasn't a glowing endorsement. Minutes later, my email chimed and there was a waiting email.

To: lmcconnell@ridgewoodcc.edu
From: jfdier@pmhs.org
Subject: re: re: Bad News

Retta-Mae doesn't know what she'd missing. I'm sure you would have been the best pet owner there was. As for dating, I know the feeling. Recently, I met someone but for one reason or another; it didn't work out. I wanted to see her again, but I guess fate, the universe, whatever you might call it, didn't agree. It's hard to be alone around the holidays.

Jeremiah F. Deir
Adoption and Foster Coordination Director
Port Madison Humane Society

PS. That guy and really, all of them were fools to let you get away.

I reread that line, over and over. While there was no way this Jeremiah guy knew Fitz, it was still nice to hear that someone out there saw, or read, my worth, even if it was only through a few brief emails. I drafted a response and then deleted it. Then rewrote it. Sitting there in my drafts, I hovered my finger over the send button before stuffing, my hands under my legs.

I wasn't sure what was drawing me to keep talking to this guy from the animal shelter. For all I knew, he was 80 years old, a great-grandfather. I shouldn't be flirting over emails with a grandfather. I didn't know any Deirs in the town, but it was such a small town that everyone knew everyone. It was possible I passed this guy all the time in line at Ridgewood Market and had no idea. He could be old or married, or old and married. Or gay. No, I didn't think he was gay. And he was definitely flirting back. Maybe.

My friends found dates on apps all the time. My roommate in college was catfished by a 14-year-old girl posing as a 6'3 rugby player once. I knew that once you add the internet into a situation, there is no way to discern the truth. But I didn't meet Jeremiah through a dating app. He accidentally emailed me from an actual place. I had been to the Humane Society before. My parents got their dog, Roscoe, there as a puppy.

Zoya peeked over my shoulder, "Girl, you know we can't have many pets here. Mr. Dawson would kill us."

Slapping my laptop closed, I narrowed my eyes at Zoya. "Snoopy much?"

Popping a section of Clementine in her mouth, Zoya shrugged. "What's so interesting about the Humane Society? If you want to pet a dog, go back to your parent's house."

Hesitating, I scratched my nose. "It's not exactly a case of wanting a pet."

A brow raised, Zoya waited for me to explain.

"I got this wrong email from a guy at the Humane Society. His name's Jeremiah. We've kind of been..."

Zoya plopped down next to me, pulling my laptop out of my hands, "Have you been sexting with some rando from the Humane Society? Lina McConnell, you tramp."

Pulling the laptop out of Zoya's hands, I held the laptop close to my chest like armor. "It's not like that. All we've done is talk. He's new to town. Mostly we chat about silly stuff like food and beer. But..."

"But there's a vibe?" There was a light behind Zoya's dark brown eyes. When I didn't respond, Zoya tilted her head to the side. "Wait, what about that guy from the Skol House? I thought you were into him."

"I told you what happened. I had a great time with him, but he checked out without so much as a note for me. He was a no-show. I have no idea when I'm going to see Fitz again. I don't know his last name or where he lives or works. If he wanted to see me again, he would have left word."

"Was that before or after you left him naked in bed to run around with a turkey hat on your head?"

I frowned at Zoya, crossing my arms. "You said you weren't going to judge me about that. I never would have mentioned my one-night stand if I knew you'd be giving me a hard time."

Zoya frowned. "I'm not giving you a hard time about sleeping with him. I saw that man and he was all sorts of fire. But not leaving your number? That is an amateur move."

Throwing my hands up, I groaned. "Because I am an amateur. The last guy I slept with was Tobin, that computer science teacher from the college."

Wrinkling her nose, Zoya shook her head. "The guy who corrected you for leaving out the T when you say often?"

Nodding, I set the laptop back down. "And cheated on me. But yes, he also corrected my grammar. I know it's dumb, but

I thought I had a connection with Fitz. It's not like it was love at first sight or anything..." Only, it almost felt that way. I could never tell my best friend that. Zoya was understanding, but to tell her I was likely in love with the man I spent a grand total of nine hours with? I would never hear the end of it. Especially if it was amounting to a big fat nothing.

I couldn't help but feel as if I would never be the same after being with Fitz, but that was ridiculous. I was a level-headed woman who had a good job and paid most of my bills on time. My car only has a few dents from opening the door into the mailbox. I ate bagged salad at least once a week, like an adult. I wasn't in love with Fitz after a single night.

"But this guy, Jeremiah, seems nice and smart. He could be 80 for all I know. Or a woman, I guess Jeremiah could be a woman's name."

"Might be." Opening up the laptop, Zoya pulled up the humane society website. "Let's find out."

I navigated to the staff information section to find little information. No picture, just a boring bio about growing up in Seattle, graduating at the top of his class five years before, a lifetime of volunteerism and animal right activism. Blah, Blah, Blah. Nothing good like does he hate rhubarb beer and love mediocre hot sauce. Zoya nudged me to the side and began scouring the Humane Society pages for mention of him, but all they found were pictures of cats, dogs, and a rabbit wearing Santa hats and a Guinea pig in a yarmulke.

They moved on to social media. She was pretty sure she found his profile; J.F. Deir with a profile picture of a guy dressed in snow gear standing on the top of a mountain with his back to the camera. It was locked up tight on private. No Instagram, no twitter, no TikTok.

"This Jeremiah Deir is a ghost." Zoya said.

"Figures." I flopped back down on the bed, staring up at the crack in the ceiling our landlord, Mr. Dawson, was supposed to fix over the summer. "All I get is ghosts these days. Ghosted by the only guy to give me an orgasm and now I can't even find a picture of someone who is probably married or has frosted tips. Oh god, what if he wears deep v-neck tee shirts? Zoya, I cannot catch feelings for a guy who wears deep v-necks. There is desperation and then there's that."

"Let's go."

I rolled my head to the side to look at Zoya. "Go where?"

Zoya stood, gathering her purse off the table, and glanced around for her keys. "To the Humane Society, of course. We'll pretend we're going to adopt a dog or something. Then we can try to catch a peek at your elusive Jeremiah."

I glanced down at my floral patterned sweatpants and over-sized 100-hour reader shirt I got from the local library. "I need to change first."

"Love you so much, Lin, but you might want to shower too." Wrinkling her nose, Zoya shooed me to the bathroom. I responded with a middle finger.

The sound of barking could be heard through the steel door. Ever the faithful best friend, Zoya took an antihistamine on the drive over. Walking into the sparse waiting room, I looked around for an office labeled "Adoption Director" or a man who could be Jeremiah. As we approached the door to the dog kennels, a head popped over the desk. For a split second, I thought it might be Jeremiah.

"Hey, Zoya Porter and Lina McConnell in my shelter." Cooper Francis said from behind the counter.

I swallowed down my disappointment at seeing our old classmate instead of the elusive Jeremiah Deir.

"What are you two ladies doing here? We're having a special right now. Twenty-five dollar adoption fees. Same application process, but cheap until next Wednesday."

"We have a small place so we'd need a small animal, a kitten maybe, or a small dog."

Cooper nodded and motioned for us to follow him. We walked down the hallway filled with various noises and smelled slightly of wetness, cleaning products, and dry kibble.

Cooper pointed at a kennel where a small white and brown dog with his back leg missing cowering in the corner. "This little guy would probably be a good fit for an apartment. His previous owners brought him in when they had to move. I know you gals, so I can vouch for you. He's shy but once he warms up, he's a good little shit."

Zoya narrowed her eyes at Cooper. "You shouldn't call that darling a little shit." Stepping forward, she placed her hands on the gate. "I want to meet him."

"Zoya." I lowered my voice to a hiss. "You're allergic."

By this time, the door had been opened and Zoya was crouched down to accept the three-legged dog who toddled over to sniff her hand. Zoya swept the dog up in her arms and the dog rested his head on her collarbone. "I don't know what you're talking about."

Scratching the little dog's head, she cooed. "We're going to change your name to Pi."

Once Zoya set her mind to something, she was determined. I knew better than to argue with her.

Back at the front of the shelter, Cooper stepped behind the counter to pull out a clipboard. "You'll have to do the paperwork with me. Our adoption director, Mr. Deir, has the rest of the day off."

Beside her, Zoya sniffed, whether it was an animal allergy sniff or something else I couldn't tell.

"Deir." I tried my best at nonchalance. "I don't recognize that name. Is he new around here?"

Copper nodded. "Yeah, he got recruited from somewhere on the Eastside a month ago. He's a cool dude. I brought him to Thanksgiving dinner with me. Nova was all over his dick the whole night. But that's just Nova. Ya know?"

"That's very interesting," Zoya said with a raised brow. I did. Cooper's cousin Nova went to school with us as well. She was petite, always immaculately dressed, and had a series of incredibly attractive boyfriends that she dumped after a few months. If Nova was attracted to this Jeremiah guy, he must be good-looking and younger.

I needed to meet this guy.

THE ONE YOU CHOSE

Fitz

T he world fell in on me at nine thirty-seven in the morning as I pulled up my emails.

To: jfdier@pmhs.org
From: emcconnell@ridgewoodcc.edu
Subject: Jeremiah

Okay, Mr. Deir, should I call you Mr. Deir or would Jeremiah work? I think at this stage of our conversations we should be on a first name basis. If I'm telling you about my dating history, you can call me by my actual name, Lina. I like getting to know you, Jeremiah. I hope I'm not overstepping, but it's surprisingly hard to connect with people these days. Maybe it's just me. I spend a lot of my days in the company of four-year-olds, who, while cute, aren't exactly challenging my conversation skills. (Though one just asked me how cows have babies. Not people, but cows.)

I hope you're not going to be alone on Christmas. Do you celebrate Christmas? I shouldn't presume. There are other holidays. Hanukkah? Kwanzaa? Rohatsi? Solstice? Whatever you celebrate, I hope you're not alone.

Some-what-embarrassedly,
Lina

I stared at the signature on the email. Lina. Could it be my Lina? Could I even call her my Lina?

And what could I say here? She only knew me as Jeremiah through the emails. I couldn't tell her now I went by Fitz, could I? What was I thinking using my first name in my work signature? It seemed like such a grown-up and professional thing to do at the time instead of my nickname and now it was biting me in the ass.

She was asking me to tell her more. How do you phrase the conversation that the person you've been talking to over email might be the same one you slept with weeks prior?

I went to Facebook and typed in McConnell. Now I could see why I couldn't find her before. Her profile picture was a group picture where she was crammed together with a bunch of people wearing hats that looked like turkeys. Her name on the profile was Evangelina McConnell. If I hadn't known what to look for, I never would have found her.

I debated on how to broach the subject. Surely this was an in-person conversation, not over email.

To: emcconnell@ridgewoodcc.edu
From: jfdier@pmhs.org
Subject: re: Jeremiah

Hi Lina,
That is a beautiful name. Just unique enough.

No, I won't be alone on Christmas. I'm going back home to see my mom for the long weekend. She has a group of friends and they all come over to the house and we make a big night of it. My Ma's friends don't have kids themselves, so it's just going to be me and a bunch of sixty-year-old aunties. It might sound weird, but I enjoy it now. (I didn't appreciate it when I was seventeen, I can tell you that.)

What about you? What do you do for the holidays?

~J

I loved learning about Lina. Connecting the stories she told me in her emails with the phenomenal women I met weeks before. Over the weeks she had told him about her family, the annoying younger brother she loved and protected. The older brother who once made her track coach cry. She told me about the kids in her classroom and how hard and yet rewarding her job was. She told me funny anecdotes about her best friend and roommate. I told her about growing up, always moving around. How I lived with my cousin for most of my freshman year while my dad was in and out of the hospital. I told her about the funny things the animals did at the shelter. How the social media manager was going to be launching a TikTok soon with the different animals. We talked and talked and I knew without a doubt that this was the woman for me.

To: jfdier@pmhs.org
From: emcconnell@ridgewoodcc.edu
Subject: re: re: Jeremiah

I'm glad you won't be alone. On Christmas Eve, my whole extended family gets together at my Aunt Cathy's house to do a gift exchange. It's wild, with at least one person ending up in tears (typically, but not always one of the children) and my other Aunt Bea getting too drunk and falling asleep by seven.

The next day I open stockings with my parents and younger brother, Payton. My older. brother, Trey and his wife, Dulcie, typically come up to join us, but Dulcie is expecting their second baby in January and he didn't want to leave her. So they're doing a small thing at their place in Phoenix.

<3 Lina

I stared at the little heart emoji next to her name. Every day, I refreshed my email, hoping for a new email from her. Knowing now that it was my Lina, made everything fit together. I just had to strategize on how to tell Lina it was me after all.

For weeks I'd think I saw her in every storefront window. The reflection of a dark-haired girl at the coffee shop, to end up wrong.

She stepped out of Sluy's Bakery, the leg of a human-shaped donut shoved in her mouth as she was stuffing her wallet into her purse. I halted, the bags of dog toys from the local pet shop banging against my legs.

Her hand shoved in her purse she looked up to see me standing in front of her. Slowly she pulled the rest of the donut out of her mouth. Her cheeks full, she smiled as she chewed.

"Hey, Lina," I said, not even trying to keep the surprise out of my voice.

"Ith!" She said, her words garbled by the donut. Chewing quickly, she swallowed down the hunk of dough. "Fitz, hi."

There were so many things I wanted to say, but I couldn't form the words. Instead, I pointed to her hand. "That's a big donut."

Real smooth talker, aren't you?

She glanced down at her mutilated treat. "Oh, yeah, they're a local thing. Dough Boys. The big controversy is, which part do you eat first? Do you eat the head and put it out of its misery or do you bite off all the limbs and let it suffer?"

"I can see what camp you're in."

She pulled off an arm of the donut and offered it to me. "What can I say? I have a bloodthirsty streak."

I popped the donut in my mouth, chewing slowly. A rush of dough goodness filled my mouth. It was quite good. A long silence stretched between us.

She motioned to the shopping bags at my legs. "Getting some last-minute shopping done?"

I trained my face to look blank. What could I say? Was this the right moment to tell her they're donations from the pet store and I'm picking them up because I work for the Humane Society? Oh, and by the way, my first name is Jeremiah.

"Uh, kind of, yeah. Just some stuff for work." I coughed and glanced over my shoulder. "Are you hungry?"

Glancing from the half-eaten donut in her hand and back up at me, she said, "Starving."

Settled into the booth at Casa Sol. I was kicking myself. The perfect opportunity to tell her who I was presented itself and

I blew it. When she asked me what I was getting downtown all I had to say was I was picking up the dog toy donation from the pet shop. A perfect chance to let her know I was Jeremiah F. Deir. Instead, I froze and lied. I was an idiot.

Lina ran a finger over the rim of her beer bottle, looking at her hand instead of at me. "I stopped by the hotel. Sandy at the front desk said you checked out."

Blinking at her, I processed that information. Sandy at the front desk gave me a shifty vibe. I should have followed up. "I didn't. I mean, I am now. But I had to move rooms. I was still there." I set my beer down as I studied her. "She didn't give you my note?"

Lina shook her head. "No. She didn't give me anything."

"But you came back?" Hope bloomed in my chest. "You tried to see me again?"

"Well, yeah." She said, before stuffing a chip in her mouth, her cheeks flaring red. She seemed to compose herself to find the words.

Leaning forward, I dropped my voice. "I wanted you to come back. I wanted to see you again."

"You did?" she asked.

Reaching across the table between us, I grabbed her hand, running my thumb over her knuckles. "I can't stop thinking about you, Lina."

Breathing heavily, a smile stretched across her face. "Same."

"When I saw you coming out of the bakery, I thought I was imagining it. Since that night, I was looking around town for you. I kept thinking I saw you for it to turn out to be someone else. I even..." Hesitating, I could feel my cheeks warm. "Um, this is embarrassing..."

Lina leaned forward. "What? Tell me what you did."

"I tried looking for you on the internet. Facebook, twitter, Instagram, all of them."

Pursing her lips together, she fought back the smile that was threatening to emerge. "Oh, it's under my full name, Evangelina. Evangelina McConnell. Or it's McLina for the fun usernames, but that would be hard to find if you didn't already know. Most of the people I have as friends on there, I've known since I was a kid." The waitress came to the table to set down the steaming plate of fajitas between us. After she left, I reached out to push the plate closer to Lina. Contact with the hot cast iron caused me to curse and jerk my hand back.

"Oh, my gosh! Are you okay?" Lina asked. Scooping ice cubes out of her water glass with her hand, she wrapped them in a napkin and held them to my hand. "Is it bad?"

I wouldn't tell her it was more shock than pain when her hand was wrapped around mine and her eyes were looking at me so tenderly. "It's better now."

A smile spread across her face. It was a smile I wanted to see for the rest of my days. I had the urge to lean across the table and kiss those soft lips.

"Tell me about your job," I asked. Her face lighting up, she regaled me with a story about a girl who insisted on decorating her paper Christmas tree with only googly eyes.

I sat back and listened, encouraging her for more stories. Before we knew it, we polished off our beers and the fajitas for two between us. She asked me a few questions, but I kept directing the conversation back at her. I knew the moment I told her things would change. I didn't want to risk it yet. Not when I just got her back.

The waitress set down the receipt between us. I grabbed the paper as Lina was reaching for it. "I'll get this one. Maybe you can buy us coffee for our next date?"

She bit the smile on her lips. "Okay, deal."

Damn, she was so pretty.

As we walked out the door, my hand drifted to the small of her back. The warmth of her body seared through her top. I watched her face as she looked up at me. I wondered if she liked the way my fingers felt on her back. Touching her brought peace to my frantic mind.

I knew I would have to confess now. I had waited too long; it was getting into a dangerous territory between omission and lies.

Exiting the restaurant, I stopped in the alley to turn to face her. "I have something to tell you, but before I do, I really want to kiss you."

Pausing, Lina must have seen the frustration lacing my brow. I took a deep breath, steadying myself in the warmth of her brown eyes. Reaching forward, I tucked a strand of dark hair into her hat. My fingers brushed along her cheekbone, sending warmth up my arm. My palm cupped the side of her face. "Could I kiss you?"

My hand still on her cheek, she gazed at me as if she couldn't imagine anything she would rather do than kiss me in that brightly painted alley. "Yes."

The kiss started slow and tender, a soft press of her lips on mine. A brushing of my tongue. Lina leaned into me, threading her arms around my neck and pulling me closer. Our bodies flush, my kiss deepened. I was losing reason. My hands roamed down her sides to rest on the small of her back. Reason was now running away as I whirled her around until her back was against the wall. My kiss more demanding now. As my body pushed into her, she moaned against my mouth. I could feel the soft lines of her.

I pulled away to stare down at her, my breath ragged. One last chance to reclaim this. "Stop, I have to tell you something."

"It can wait." She pulled my face to hers. Her kiss as demanding as the lust thrumming through me. I needed more. My mouth left hers and she gasped in air as my lips traveled down her neck. Tilting her head to the side to give me better access, my teeth scraping against the soft flesh of her throat. "Where's your place?"

"Just up the hill, by the brewery." My words muffled by her skin.

"Take me home. Take me to bed." I pulled away to stare down at her, then took her hand and lead her out the alleyway and into the bustling holiday crowd.

The key got stuck in the lock, and I had to jiggle it several times to get the door opened. All the while, Lina was kissing my neck, running her hand down my chest, pushing her curves against my body. Once the door swung open, we tumbled in. Scarves and hats flung on the floor as I walked her back into the bedroom. Lina's boots ended up resting beside a box labeled "dishes and shit" and my coat flung upside down on a half-assembled desk.

Lina's knees hit the bed, and I steadied her. Stepping back, I gripped the bottom of her sweater, dragging it over her head. My shirt was on the ground somewhere between the hallway and bedroom. My fingers gripped the zipper of her jeans and she nodded at the question in my eyes. The sound of the zipper teeth loud beside our heavy breaths, she kicked the jeans off her legs. As I watched her, I pulled off my jeans. Her eyes on me, Lina reached behind her back to unclasp her bra, letting it fall down between us.

My eyes raked over her body. I liked what I saw. Reaching out I ran a finger over her collarbone, her skin warm under my touch. "So many nights I've thought that you couldn't be this perfect, that I made it up in my head, but you look even better than I remembered. You are spectacular." Tracing a line down her bare skin from her collarbone to the swell of her breast, I watched my hand.

Reaching forward, her fingers traveled down my chest to the spot above my hips. "If we could have remembered it, it would have hurt that much more."

"I'm never forgetting this moment. Your skin under my fingers and the way your body is reacting to me. For as long as I live, I'll never forget this." I stepped closer and together we fell back onto the bed. I could feel every part of her softness as her hips came up to meet me. "Tell me you want this as much as I do."

She cupped her hand around the back of my neck, holding my face still. "I want it more. I want it all."

My lips descended on hers and I showed her how much I wanted her.

WHOSE ARMS WILL HOLD YOU

Lina

H is fingers on my skin sent sparks through my body. Heavy on top of me as he kissed me, his tongue urging into my mouth. All over my body felt scorched from him. He both soothed the ache deep inside me and set me aflame.

His mouth left mine as he trailed down my throat, the cold air delicious against the wetness of his kiss. His teeth scraped the sensitive skin of my collarbone. Pulling up slightly, one of his hands cupped my breast. I looked down to watch as his thumb rubbed a circle against my nipple.

"How are you this perfect?" he asked, his voice so soft I wondered if he meant the question for me or himself. He glanced up at me, his warm brown eyes on mine. "Look how you fit me. Do you feel this too?"

If I had never met him, I wouldn't have known how good this would feel. Blissful ignorance to this level of passion and heat.

I nodded at him. "Yes, I feel it."

His gaze settled on my breasts, watching the flush under his touch. "This is crazy, I barely know you but this, you--"

His mouth closed over my nipple, his words dying on his tongue. I arched beneath him as he teased and sucked. With his other hand he pushed my underwear down, his finger grazing a circle around my clit.

"Jesus, you are so wet." He parted my folds as his thumb worked my clit and then his fingers were inside me, sliding against my walls.

My fingers clutched the back of his neck as he moved inside me. I was going to come from his fingers alone. I couldn't even do that to myself, but he was going to do it for me. He worked me over, his pace never lessening. I squirmed against his hand, needing more of him while crying out, *right there, yes, more, yes, right there.*

All the while I was barreling closer to climax he watched my face, a smile playing at his lips. Throwing my head back, my hands scrambled for purchase on his back, my short nails scratching him as I crested.

"That's it." He coaxed. "Come all over my hand."

Gripping his shoulders I felt myself fall apart. His fingers moving inside me, draining every drop of pleasure from me.

Resting my head on his shoulder, my arms loosened from their grip around him. He moved back to my mouth, his kisses reverent on me.

"Before we go any further, I want to be very clear. I want you to stay the night. I want to make you breakfast in the morning and I want your number in my phone and your picture as my lock screen. Do you understand?"

Opening my eyes, I nodded at him, surprised by the wetness that was threatening to overflow in my eyes. Swallowing down the sudden burst of emotion in my throat, I stroked his cheek. "I want that too. I want you."

With my words, he kissed me again. His hands coming down to grip my ass and pull me around him. I heard the crinkle of a wrapper and then he was between my thighs. I grabbed his ass, pulling him inside me. Wrapping my legs around him, he thrust inside me, filling me up. Gasping at the sensation of him, my eyes snapped open to find him looking down at me. A small smile ticked up on his face as he moved inside me. The dimple on the left side of his cheek deepening. I remembered the first time I saw that dimple. Bringing my hand up, I cupped his cheek, the dimple resting beneath my thumb. This is what I wanted that night. Our eyes on each other, his hands on my body, feeling him inside me.

"This is perfect, you feel so good," he murmured against my skin as we moved together, edging closer and closer and then falling together.

An hour later, fully sated after three orgasms, I rolled over onto my side, propped up by my elbow. Beside me, Fitz had his arm over his head, his eyes closed and a blissed out look on his face. I bent down and pressed a kiss to his lips before getting up to use the bathroom.

He had one of those mirrors with the medicine cabinet behind it. Being a little snoopy wasn't a polite thing to do, but he was just balls deep inside me, so I figured I could poke around a little. There was a tube of deodorant, a bottle of pain reliever, and a half full box of bandages with a tube of antibiotic ointment in it. Surprisingly boring stuff.

Coming out, I veered to the kitchen to get myself a glass of water. It was a small place. From my spot at the counter, I could see through the open doorway to the foot of his bed. He hadn't put curtains up yet and the late afternoon light trickled through the living room window. Faint shadows cast against the blank white walls and his television. I could hear the low sound of a car driving down the street and the thrumming bass of the stereo as it passed.

Setting the glass of water down on the counter, I glanced around his place. He hadn't seemed to make much progress in unpacking, but it had only been a few weeks in his new place. My scarf was hanging off the edge of the table, from where I had tossed it an hour before. Walking over, I grabbed the scarf to fold it. Underneath was a blue and yellow lanyard with Port Madison Humane Society printed on it. I picked up the lanyard. On the end was an ID badge with the name Jeremiah F. Deir on it.

The plastic badge was cold in my hand as I read then reread the name, trying to figure out how Fitz's picture could be on this badge. It didn't make any sense, he couldn't be the same guy. He wouldn't do that to me, would he? Tightening my grip until the edges scored my palm, I realized I didn't know Fitz at all. In a shaky voice, I called out. "Fitz. Come here."

Stepping out of the bedroom with only his boxers on, Fitz glanced from my face to the lanyard in my hand. "Give me a minute to explain," he said. "It's not what it looks like."

My voice was low and quiet. "I don't understand. Why does it say Jeremiah Deir on here?"

His jaw tightened, and he gave a long sigh. "Because that's my name."

"So you lied to me. You told me your name is Fitz, but it's *Jeremiah. Jeremiah?*" I enunciated each part of his first name as if it were a curse.

"Yeah, Jeremiah *Fitzgerald* Deir."

My brow raised as I stared at him, a red fury behind my eyes. "Did you know?"

He gulped. I didn't need to finish the question. "I just realized a week ago. When told me your name."

"We've been talking for weeks and you didn't think to mention that you are the guy I slept with? You didn't think to mention that before we slept together *again?* Was that a joke to you? Am I? You may sleep with a ton of anonymous women but *I don't do that.*"

"I don't either." Fitz put his hands up in surrender. "I swear. When you first emailed me, I had no way of knowing that you were the same person. Your email starts with an E. It wasn't until you told me your name that the pieces clicked together. I was trying to figure out a way to tell you, but everything I thought of felt wrong. And I tried to tell you at the restaurant, but then I kissed you and it was like my head stopped working. All I could think about was being with you again."

"I can't believe you. There is no way I could believe another word that comes out of your mouth." I paced between the table and the counter, the lanyard still clenched painfully in my hand. "Here I was thinking what we had was special, that it was fate that brought us back together tonight, but now, I don't believe in anything."

I turned to walk away, and Fitz caught my upper arm, holding me still. "Please, give me another chance. It was a stupid miscommunication."

Shaking him off, I glared. "It was a miscommunication a week ago. Now it's deception. I told you; I don't like liars. Let go of me."

He dropped my arm and I stalked away. Grabbing my clothes, I pulled on only what was necessary and carried the rest in my arms.

As I dressed, he pleaded with me. "Lina, I never meant to lie to you. I'm shit at talking to people. Awkward conversations are my worst nightmare. I had no idea how to bring it up, but I never meant to deceive you. Please, stop so I can explain."

"The moment I gave you my full name you should have told me the truth. Not let this drag on for days. A week. Not let me make a fool of myself..."

"You never were foolish."

"I don't want to hear another word."

"You never told me your full name. I never told you mine. We both got caught up. Please, I need you to stay. Since the first time I saw you, all I wanted was to get to know you. Please don't leave like this."

Shaking my head, I squinched my eyes shut. He could see me gulping for air. "I needed you too. For weeks, I needed so desperately to believe that what we had was special, but now? Your lies? You've shattered me."

I could feel his eyes on my back as I walked out the door. Waiting until the door slammed behind me, I felt the tears welling up in my eyes. I didn't want him to chase after me or hear his explanations. The thunder of being played the fool arced through my body. How could I have believed that fate had brought us together when all it seemed to do was tear me apart?

AMONG THE MISSING

Lina

I woke up the next morning with the email in my inbox. I deleted it without looking further than the subject line. Even after putting my phone down, I could see his name. The F in his address. All the facts he sprinkled through our correspondence. Every time that he told me exactly who he was and I was too blind to see it.

Laying my hands over my sternum I pressed into myself, urging the ache to recede. When I thought of Fitz, it was as if my chest was cracking open. That first night together it was as if a part of me had unlocked. I wanted more. I needed more. And now all I had was the desolation of being without.

"Wait, so the veterinarian you've been flirting with and Fitz from the bar are the same guy?" Zoya asked as she scratched behind Pi's ear. The dog wasted no time in making himself at home on the couch. After bringing him home, we both waited for Zoya's allergies to kick in but so far there was no sign of even a sniffle. After a week, Zoya asked her doctor if she grew out of her allergy to animals to find that she was never actually allergic and it was a story her parents told her growing up because they didn't want animals in their home. Zoya stopped talking to her mother for six days, a record in the Porter family.

"He's not a veterinarian; he's the adoption and foster coordinator. His job is to make sure that the animals are placed in the right homes."

Zoya flapped her hand as if swatting a fly. "Whatever. The point is, they're the same guy?"

I nodded. "There's no point in reading it."

"He might have a good reason or even a dumb reason."

"It's a huge red flag. There's never a good reason to lie." That first night, I told him. I couldn't do liars. He knew and he still lied to me.

Rolling her eyes, Zoya sat up. "You are being ridiculous. Yes, the circumstances are ridiculous. But when was he supposed to tell you? Through email? You're acting like it was some great deception to get into your pants."

"It was! I slept with him, again, before I found out the truth."

"So he maliciously tried to hide the truth from you?"

"Well, not maliciously." I edged.

"And he didn't try to tell you the truth at any point?"

I thought back to the alleyway. My hands on his hair and the way he pulled away; pleading that he had something to tell me. He could have told me then, but if he was feeling the same lust-driven heat that I was, his mind wasn't on conversation. "There might have been a moment..."

Her voice softened, Zoya reached out and took my hand. "I know how you feel about lying. But something like this, it's not all black and white. There is no hard and fast rule when you're falling for someone."

I wanted to argue with her, but what could I say? Never before had I felt this way over a man. I wanted to curse him; I wanted to lie beside him and never get up. To never see his face again and to trace the contours of his cheek with my fingers. Simply put, I was out of my depth.

Zoya snapped her fingers. "Give me your phone."

"I deleted the email." Which was half true. It was still sitting in my trash folder but not permanently deleted. I couldn't bring myself to do that yet. Zoya would know this too. Zoya scoffed and snapped her finger impatiently. Handing my phone to Zoya, I covered my eyes.

Zoya read the email aloud as I buried my face in our "There's some Ho-Ho-Ho's in this house" pillow.

To: emcconnell@ridgewoodcc.edu
From: jfdeir@pmhs.org
Subject: Please

Lina,

I have no right to ask this. But I can't help but ask for one more chance. I never meant to deceive you. Everything I said at the restaurant, I meant. I can't stop thinking of you. The night we met, the first time I saw you, it was as if everything around you vanished for me. You are kind, and smart, and beautiful. Never in my life did I think I would find a connection with another person the way I did with you. I never wanted to hurt you, and if you'll give us a chance, I'd like to make it up to you. Please.

I won't send you anymore emails. On New Year's Eve, I'm going to be at your tree downtown at nine. I'll wait all night if I have to. If you want to start over, I'll be waiting for you.
~Fitz

Jeremiah F. Deir

Adoption Coordination Director
Port Madison County Humane Society

Zoya tossed the phone back down beside me. "Doesn't sound like a guy who was trying to deceive you, he just sounds bad at communicating, which isn't great. But it's also not bad enough to never see him again if you really care about him. If this guy just wanted a hookup, he could have chosen a ton of other girls, didn't Cooper say his cousin Nova was trying to get with him?"

Turning my head to the side I frowned at her. "What's your point."

"He's putting in some work for you. If you were just some piece of ass for him, would he really be saying all this?"

"I don't know," I grumbled.

Flopping down on the couch beside me, Zoya picked up my legs and draped them over her lap. "Neither do I, but you have a little over a week to decide."

WHAT ARE YOU DOING

Fitz

O n my mother's front door hung the largest and most ornate wreath I had ever seen. Balancing the wreath that I bought for her in one hand, I closed the door to my car. Before I left town, my mother had asked me to get a wreath from Garden of Eden Nursery in Ridgewood. Apparently, it was consistently rated the best nursery in the area and made unique arrangements that had been featured in magazines and online. I couldn't tell the difference, but I did as my mother asked, buying a wreath and some bulb plant called an amaryllis from a younger man ridiculously named, Thorne Eden.

Before I could get to the front door, my mother poured out onto the porch with her friends on her heels. "Baby! What took you so long? You were supposed to be here an hour ago. I've been cooking your Christmas favorites all day."

"You have not, Suzette." Her friend, Alvita shook her head. "You've been sitting at the table with a glass of wine and complaining about that neighbor of yours while I've been cooking."

My mom shrugged. "Well, someone's been cooking all day." Taking the duffel bag from my shoulder she wrapped her arms around me, pulling me close to her body. The familiar scent of cherry blossom scented lotion on her skin. No matter how old I got, having a hug from my mother was one of the best feelings in the world. Pulling away she studied my face. "You look tired. How are you sleeping, have you been taking that melatonin? Because I told you, it's only for a little while. I sent you that article didn't I..."

As she kept on about the recommended dosage of herbal remedies for sleep, I trailed behind her into the house. A Christmas tree was set up in the corner of the living room with a few boxes underneath the tree. As a child we used to go out every year and pick out our own tree from a farm, my father would hold his hand over mine as we sawed through the trunk and my mother would take a photo of us, calling us her strapping men. This tree was smaller than the ones we used to get, but of course, she had no one to chop it down for her now.

"Oh that," my mother came in following my eye line. "A neighbor brought that over, they had an extra."

"Ma, I could have got you a tree."

She raised a brow and made some noncommittal sound. Message received.

"Or I could have helped pay for it, at least."

"Absolutely not. I am your mother and I take care of you. Now, go scoot upstairs and get changed, you can't wear that dirty tee shirt for Christmas dinner." I glanced down at my shirt, it was the same one I wore the night I met Lina, a screen print of one of artist Lisandre's more popular works. I touched the red shirt, remembering the way she looked at me in it. The feel of her hand in mine as we walked away together. How badly I fucked everything up with her.

My mother pushed my back towards the stairs, and I feigned protest for a moment before relenting. She missed bossing me around, I could tell.

Making my way through the house, I was surprised to see a few changes since I had been there months earlier. After my father passed, the memories we had in our old house was too much for her. She bought a new place a decade before but still filled the house with mementos from my father. There were my father's books on the shelf, lined up by dates of publication. Our family picture in the same spot on the staircase. My father standing awkwardly behind my mother with his hand placed on her shoulder, while I squirmed on her lap. A picture of me sitting on my grandfather's lap, my father next to us. Three generations of Jeremiah Fitzgerald Deirs. Their wedding quilt still hung on the wall of the dining room. But the literary awards that used to line the study walls were replaced by oil paintings. The old recliner my father loved was replaced with a plush leather chair where my cat Hank was sleeping. He opened one disdainful gold eye then shut it. He must have missed me a lot.

My room was exactly the way it looked when I lived there. The wrestling trophies on the bookshelf next to James Baldwin, Gary Paulsen, and Jack London. The camouflage print comforter and a poster of my favorite rapper from my high school years. I tried to put up a poster of a scantily clad pop star once, but after an hour I found the poster was missing. My mother told me I was lucky all she did was throw it away.

Sitting on the twin bed, I imagined what Lina would think of the room. Of my mother. I could picture it so clearly, the way she would greet my mom. She would be nervous at first, then only minutes in she'd talk about her classroom and my mother would be charmed. My mother would have loved Lina.

After a long Christmas dinner of all my favorite foods, my mother's friends left back to their houses. I called Alvita an uber since she had a few too many glasses of Cabernet. I walked my mother's other friend, Trisha, the three blocks home. The area was relatively safe but it didn't feel right for her to walk alone in the dark.

As I walked back to my mother's house I stuffed my hands in my pockets to keep warm. The streets were ones I walked down many times as a child, but I never felt at home in the neighborhood. My mom was always busy with work. There were few kids my age on the street. Four years I lived at that house with my mom and it never felt the way my bungalow in Ridgewood felt.

When I returned from the blustery night, my mom had filled my wineglass with the rest of the bottle. "Now that those busybodies are gone, tell me about the girl."

I tapped my thumb on the stem of the glass. "Who says there's a girl?"

Pursed lips, my mom raised a single brow. "You think I don't know my son? The way you're mooning around here? Only a woman can do that to a man. You're just like your father. Weeks and weeks I made him wait around before I went out with him. He had that same look on his face every time I saw him. So, stop bullshitting your Momma and tell me about her."

Hesitating, I covered my mouth with a hand. My mother could see through me. It had been like this since I was a child. The few times I tried to misbehave my Ma knew before I got home. For so many years after my father passed it had only been the two of us.

"Her name is Lina. She's a preschool teacher in Ridgewood."

"And where is this Lina now? Why didn't you bring her over here?"

I scrubbed a hand over my face, the two-day-old stubble rough on my palm. I should have shaved for my mom. "It didn't, I mean we didn't work out."

"What did you do?" my mother sat back, crossing her arms over her chest.

"What makes you think I did anything?"

Arms still crossed, my mother was silent. Point taken.

"I may have been a little less than forthcoming about who I was."

My mother made a dangerous "mmhmmm" sound that echoed my childhood memories of being in trouble. I explained what happened as best I could, leaving out the late-night details of our two meetings. I was not about to talk about sex with my mom.

"I wrote her another email asking her for another chance, but I don't know if she'll respond, she was mad."

"Because you're acting like a fool." My mother shook her head. "I didn't raise my son to be like that. You know better."

I nodded. After emailing Lina, I realized she wouldn't respond. In the small town we were bound to run into each other again. I knew it was likely a lost cause. She had told me that first night she didn't like liars.

I shooed my mom away to the living room, while I started handwashing the dishes. My mother refused to get a dishwasher, insisting that she could clean it better than an old machine. Hank, my cat slinked around my ankles, hoping for a spare piece of food to be dropped on the ground. My hands deep in hot soapy water I heard the back door click open. In the doorway was an older gentleman holding a bottle of wine in one hand and a wrapped gift in the other. I dried my hands on the dishtowel, studying the man. He was close to my mother's age, with salt and pepper hair and tan skin. He was dressed in a red and green flannel. I looked from the man to my mother. There was a scrambling sound from the other room and my mother was in the kitchen again.

"Oh, Domingo." My mother stepped between them, fumbling with her wineglass. Her eyes darted from the gentleman to me. "Uh, Domingo, this is my son, Fitz."

To the man's credit, he smoothly set the wine down and stuck his hand out to me. "Domingo Garza. I've heard a lot about you from your mother."

Taking the man's hand, I shot my mother a quick look. "Is that so?"

"Domingo moved in next door about six months ago. He is the principal at the middle school. He showed me how to train my cucumbers to grow on the trellis last summer."

I got the feeling a lot more than the upkeep of creeping vines was going on. The man had a firm handshake and apparently a good job. It had been ten years since my father passed. I wasn't going to tell my mother what to do.

After a minute of awkward conversation, I excused myself, heading up the stairs to hide in my room like I did when I was fifteen. Some things never change when you go home.

C hristmas was as loud and busy and warm as I knew it would be. My little cousin accidentally kicked a hole in my father's antique stereo. Uncle Chester got sent to no-man's-land of the garage after pinching Aunt Bea's middle and commenting that she was looking "tubby." My mother grumbled the whole time about how many people were in her home even though she was the one who insisted on hosting Christmas Eve dinner every year. I was two glasses deep of oinomelo, a mulled honey wine, and dusk was falling outside in shades of muted pink and orange. A dull drizzle painted the streets outside with a shine. As it was almost every year in the Pacific Northwest, a white Christmas was unlikely. For some reason we got good snow storms in February typically a week after everyone got their snow tires taken off. Glancing out the window I saw their neighbor's, The Pryce's, had set up a large outdoor Christmas display of tasteful wire animals lit with small lights. Not to be outdone by Janine Pryce, my mother had my father on the roof for hours setting up their display; the whole of Avonwood Ponds illuminated by the thousands of lights on their roof. The week before, Santa had ridden by on the fire truck, handing out candy canes with the help of elves, a local tradition put on by the fire department.

Taking a sip of my mulled honey wine, I thought back to the holidays before this one. All the same. The bickering between sisters, the kids getting into trouble, the husbands hiding in the garage listening to whatever sport was playing on the radio. Yia-Yia sat in the corner sipping her white wine and eating pistachios. I loved my family and the holidays, but I couldn't get rid of the ache in my chest. I grabbed a melomakarona off the plate, munching on the honey cookie to soothe the pangs shuddering through me.

No matter that this holiday was one of my favorites, I couldn't stop wondering where Fitz was, and if he truly meant what he said in his email. From my wallowing spot in a chair, I watched as they opened gifts, ate dinner, and reveled together in holiday spirit. I feigned a smile or two, but couldn't muster much more.

"Darling, what is wrong with you?" My mother asked, frowning as she looked from the frown on my face, to my empty wineglass, to the cookie crumbs scattered over the front of my scarlet velvet dress.

"Nothing."

"Evangelina, I know when you are lying. What's going on?"

I opened my mouth to make an excuse and began to cry.

Ten minutes later we were hiding out in her bedroom, sitting on her California King with its white and blue floral comforter. My hands clutching a big mug of steamy tea, I told her the story as best I could. The way we met after I was stood up, the missed connection the next day. The emails we sent each other and the growing intimacy of our communication. Seeing him again to find out he was the same man I was emailing this entire holiday season. The only thing I left out was the gory details of our nights together. She didn't need to hear that.

"... and everything about us felt like fate pulling me to him only to rip us apart. To see him again that way, it felt like it was meant to be. But to find out he lied? I don't know if I can forgive him for that, Mama."

My mother pulled my hands in hers. Looking down at our joined fingers I noticed the way her pinkies had a slight curve the same as mine.

"I don't love that you spent the night with a man, but I won't say anything more." Her face soured as if she wanted to say more, but was martyring herself on the alter of restraint. "Maybe this is fate, maybe not. But what it can be is an opportunity. What is your heart telling you to do? Not that sweet rational head, but your heart?"

I paused as I thought about her question. Why did I want to assume the worst of Fitz for not telling me? I knew my answer. It had been the same since that night at the bar when he took my hand in his and led me away from the crowd.

He fit me. We fit together. I craved him. For the first time in my life, I felt seen, heard. It didn't matter that we only spent a few hours together. What we had was special. I couldn't let that go over a misunderstanding, could I?

When I didn't answer, my mother patted my hand. She must have known that I didn't have a good answer. "Why don't you sleep here tonight? Daddy will make you Christmas breakfast in the morning."

Taking a large gulp of the tea, I felt the scalding liquid burn my tongue. Great, now I'd have a sore tongue, a hangover and a broken heart in the morning. Nothing but great decisions tonight.

My mother said nothing, leaving me in my self-pity.

I moved to my childhood bedroom. My parents hadn't changed it much. They switched out the bedding for less flashy stuff; I was going through a neon color phase the last time I lived here. My yellowing old Babysitters Club and Fear Street paperbacks lined up on the high bookshelf. My mother took down the collage I made of male celebrities and put up a landscape of Oia.

I changed into a pair of silk pajamas my mother gave me, an ornate set that I would never buy for myself. My pajamas were old-school tee shirts and ratty athletic shorts. Downstairs I could hear my parents and brother watching It's a Wonderful Life. We watched the holiday movie together every Christmas. All day long the next day, my mother would chide my father with the line "George, why must you torture the children" to all of our raucous laughter. I knew they'd be wondering where I was but I couldn't bring myself to join them. Out the window, I watched as Aunt Cathy shooed her kids to the car, yelling that if they didn't get in St. Basil wasn't going to bring them any presents. They listened to that.

Sliding between the high thread count sheets I closed my eyes. Christmas would come and then New Year's after that. Turning to my side, I allowed myself to wonder what it would feel like to have Fitz by my side.

Viscount Rodolphe had stolen a phaeton from another man and was currently racing across Mayfair to tell Lady Beatrice how he felt. He knew how to woo a woman. I pictured Fitz in a cravat, the two-wheeled vehicle careening as he raced to my side. Me in a low-cut dress, my fichu barely covering me as I waited for my lover.

"You sure you don't want to come with us?" Zoya fixed a pin in her dark intricate updo that likely took her hours.

I set down my book to study Zoya. When I told her I wasn't going out for New Year she invited me out to the masquerade party in Manzanita. While it was a kind offer, I knew Milo had gotten the tickets for it weeks before and even if I wanted to come, there was no chance I could get in.

Since the email, Zoya was careful not to ask too often about what I was going to do. Careful for her at least, which meant she only asked me once a day. True restraint, that woman.

"No, I'll drink a bottle of cheap champagne and watch the countdown at the Space Needle on TV like all the other losers out there."

"Don't drink alone. At least go to the Skol House if you're going to be pathetic."

"Love you too, Zo." I stuck my tongue out.

Zoya pinched my cheek playfully. "And you're not going to see him?"

"I haven't decided yet."

Milo knocked before opening the front door. He had a key to our place and was always careful not to walk in without knocking, likely a holdover from having a stepsister his age.

"You ready?" he asked Zoya before looking at me. I could see the surprise in his eyes as he took in my Stained Ridgewood Baseball tee shirt I stole years before from my brother and the oversized sweatpants that my ex-boyfriend left behind a year before.

"Oh, hey, Lina. You good?" his question falling off at the end. As he fumbled for words, Zoya raced around the room looking for her lost wallet.

"Peachy, Milo. So peachy." Standing, I picked up a pile of magazines that were hiding her wallet. I handed it to her. "You two better get going, you don't want to be late."

"Are you sure you don't want to come?" Zoya asked one more time and I could see Milo raise a brow in fear. Quickly I let him out of his misery.

"Absolutely not. You two go, have fun. I bet your car is waiting for you." I pushed her towards the door.

Once they had left, I walked to the fridge, pulling out the bottle of champagne I snagged from my parent's pantry a few days prior. Popping the cork, I took a swallow straight from the bottle. The cold sweet liquid went down easily.

Too easily. Pulling the bottle away I checked the label. Sparkling Apple Cider. Non-Alcoholic. Dammit. That would not do. If I was going to be a wallowing idiot alone on New Year, I was going to do it drunk.

Grumbling, I changed out of my old sweatpants and shirt and into slightly more presentable clothes, which I then covered with my rain jacket and boots. Getting into my cold car, I turned on the heat, letting the musty warm air flow over my face for a minute before I made the five-minute drive to Ridgewood Market. The radio was playing some old holiday standard. Outside my window, the lights of Front Street reflected off the dark wet pavement. I could still meet Fitz. It was only seven and he said he'd wait all night. I wanted so badly to believe in what I felt with him, but what if I was wrong? If it hurt this bad after two nights together how hard would it be if it didn't work out later? How did I know he really wanted to be with me?

In the store, I double-checked that the bottle I grabbed did indeed contain enough alcohol to last me through the night. ThenNi grabbed a second bottle, just in case.

I made my way to the sandwich counter to order my favorite, a jambon and brie baguette. Despite the twelve-dollar price tag price I bought it for myself without a second thought. Was it bland? Yes. But after the week I had, I didn't want spice.

I couldn't even bring myself to put hot sauce on my mac and cheese the day before. Bland food and my books, my solace. The buzz of the grocery store around me was a low roar as I made my way to the check-out stand.

Pausing in the sweets aisle, I picked up a bag of my favorite dark chocolate dipped cookies. This trip was proving to be an expensive pity party, but I was past caring. Black boots stopped in front of me and I looked up to see Sandy from the hotel. Her arms crossed over her chest and glared at me.

"Sandy," I glanced around to ensure she was stopping to talk to me and not trying to get the same overpriced cookies as me. "Hi, how are you? What are you doing here?"

Sandy frowned at me, a line forming between her brows. She wore a thick black coat over a green polo I recognized as the same one she wore that day in the hotel. White fluff was sticking out of a small hole at the bottom of her coat. "Look, I saw you up here and while I know we've had our differences, or whatever, I thought you should have this."

Reaching in her quilted purse she pulled out a square of paper with the name <u>Lina</u> on it in neat block letters. She tossed the paper on the display of sugar cookies between us.

I picked it up, unfolding it to find it was from Fitz.

Lina,

They're having me change rooms. I'm in 147 now. I hope you'll come to see me or give me a call so we can see each other again. I had a great time and I'd really like to see you again.

-Fitz (Dier, I think I forgot to tell you last night)

His phone number was on the bottom. He wanted me to stay. He was telling the truth about that.

I looked up from the paper to see Sandy scowling at me.

"Why didn't you give me this when I stopped by?" I asked, trying in vain to keep the annoyance out of my voice.

She shrugged. "Walter wrote Regina on the envelope he put it in. And honestly, you've never liked me, so I wasn't going to go out of my way and invade a guest's privacy to help you with your little booty calls. It might not be that impressive to someone like you, but I like my job."

"Who says I don't like you?" Studying her, I tried to figure out what it was. When I was a child, I remember coming home to my mother crying because one of the other girls in my school, Tracy Penrose, told me my hair made me look like Mickey Mouse. Whatever that meant. Even if I didn't like people, I wanted them to like me. It was dumb but true. The same feeling came rushing back to me with Sandy. I didn't really know her but I wanted her to like me. This desperation was an ugly thing. "I don't know why you would think that. I like you."

Sandy rolled her eyes at me. "Whatever. We're adults, I don't need you to be my friend. I was just feeling guilty about not giving this to you so I stuck it in my purse in case I saw you."

Refolding the note I placed it inside my wallet beside a picture of my niece. Sandy was now shrugging her purse over her shoulder in an attempt to leave.

"Thank you." It wasn't her fault, not really. It was no-one's.

That made all this worse. I knew I couldn't blame Fitz alone for the misunderstanding. Could he have told me earlier, sure. But I was the one who left that morning with no notice.

Sandy shot me a sarcastic wave before leaving me alone with a month-old note, two bottles of cheap champagne, and my regrets.

Fingering the note, I knew what I had to do.

NEW YEAR'S EVE

Fitz

I showed up at the brewery early enough that they were still serving people. Lina's tree was away from the heat lamps, but I didn't care. I sat down beneath her tree, my amber beer in one hand and my phone in the other. It was now a waiting game of whether Lina would show up. If being true to my word was going to be the only way she'd trust me again, I was going to do that. I wasn't going to leave until the next morning, if I took that long.

Nine forty-five rolled around and my toes were getting cold in their wool socks and boots. I stashed a thermos of hot coffee in the bag at my feet, but I didn't want to pull that out until the owner closed up shop. Across the rain-soaked road the Skol House was getting busy, with revelers showing their ID to the temporary bouncer at the door. The bright flashing beer signs in the window advertising the latest spiked seltzer. The sounds of early aughts hip-hop trickled into the street, so loud I could feel the bass. I knew inside the bar, the air would be heavy with sweat, spilled beer, and too much cologne. But out on the patio of the brewery, the air was crisp and cold. I could smell the brine of Freedom Bay and dirt of the streets.

"Hey man, I got to close up." Kat, the owner and "beer-tender" came out to tell me. We had spoken a few days before about the likelihood the Sonics would come back to Seattle, (prognosis, unlikely) and the best place to mountain bike in the area. She had recently gotten a rescue from the Humane Society, a lab-pit bull mix named Dane, that was sleeping in his bed in the corner. She told me earlier that her and Dane were going to a party in nearby Illahee to ring in the new year.

I handed her my empty glass and motioned to the outside area. "Is it okay if I hang out here? I was kind of waiting on someone."

Hesitating, she glanced around as if there was someone around listening. "Okay, but I have to lock my doors, so don't go peeing on my bushes or anything."

Watching as she locked up the small brewery, the lights going out on the brewing equipment in the back until the only light was a small one above the bar. She whistled for her dog and they both climbed into her truck to drive away. Without the lights of the brewery on, the patio was a dark wash of indigo sky and charcoal streets.

As I grabbed the hot coffee out of my bag, I ignored the bottle of champagne and two plastic flutes I bought at the party store. These were hopeful purchases. Screwing off the top of the thermos, I drank from the lip, not bothering to pour it out into the small cup lid. The cold air was biting into my legs now. I had long since lost feeling in my toes, but I would be true to my word. Lina deserved that.

An hour later, the music in the Skol House hadn't changed much, but there were two fights on the sidewalk to keep me entertained. Apparently, some blonde-haired man had hit on a guy's girlfriend. Twenty minutes later, a girl came running out of the bar with two friends at her heels crying about cheating douche-bags. A minute after that a beefy-looking man followed behind her yelling that it wasn't what it looked like.

I checked the time on my phone. 11:17. Less than an hour until the new year. After drinking the entire thermos, nature was beginning to call. I had promised Kat that I wouldn't pee on her bushes but the only place I could use was the Skol House. At the door, the bouncer made me pay a fifteen-dollar cover charge to come in even after I exclaimed, I only wanted to use the bathroom. My need won out and handed the money over, rushing to the back corner room as fast as I could through the crowd. I saw Cooper's cousin Nova being hit on by some guy and walked faster, not wanting to talk with her.

Once I was back outside, I walked past the bouncer and back to the brewery. Approaching the chair, I was in I stopped in my tracks as a figure turned at the sound of my footsteps. My breath caught in my throat as I looked at Lina. She wore a red hat, pulled down over her long dark hair. I couldn't tell if she was wearing a dress or pants under her long grey wool coat. She was a vision of red, black and grey before me.

"You came," I asked more than stated as if he couldn't believe I was there either.

"I did." She stuffed her gloved hands in the pocket of her jacket and stepped closer to me.

If she came that meant she at least wanted to see me, to talk, something. It was a good sign and one I wasn't going to take for granted.

I took another step closer. If I reached out my hand, I could have touched her, but I needed her to know this was at her pace. I was beholden to only her. "I've been waiting for you. I would have waited all night for you."

"I know that. I got your note you left." Her voice was low. "I wanted him to be you."

I waited for her to continue talking. Down the street, I could hear the shouts of revelers emptying onto Front Street. She stepped closer, her hands folding in front of her. "When we were emailing. When I knew you as Jeremiah. I wished he could have been you."

"He is me." One more step and my jacket brushed against hers. "From the moment I saw you, I knew you were it for me. I can't describe it. I don't have a clue what the future holds, but I need you beside me."

She leaned forward, resting her forehead against mine. Her voice wavered and I could tell she felt just as nervous as I did. "Tell me something embarrassing."

Our eyes closed; I reveled in having her so close to me. "When I was seven, I didn't think anyone else was dressing up for their first communion pictures and I cried so hard when my babysitter put me in my suit that my face looked like I had an allergic reaction."

"Do you still have the picture?"

I chuckled. "My mom framed it. It's next to the wedding photo of her and my Pops."

"I can't wait to see it."

I took in a deep breath. "Does this mean you'll give me another shot?"

"I want to. So badly. But..." She hesitated.

Steeping closer to her, I took her hand in mine. I started with her pinky, slowly pulling each finger out of her glove until her hand was bare. Shoving the glove in my pocket, I pulled her hand up to my mouth, pressing my lips to the soft warm skin above her knuckles. Her eyes huge as she took in my motions, I took the moment of her losing words to speak. "Someone once told me that New Year's is a chance for a fresh start. To create more for yourself. To fall in love."

Her breath hitched at her words being repeated back to her. "I've heard that before too."

Studying her hand, I laced our fingers together, turning her wrist until we were connected. "So, hi, nice to meet you. I'm Jeremiah Fitzgerald Deir, the fourth."

"Fitzgerald? That name is a mouthful."

"Now you see why I go by Fitz. The rest are family names. My dad went by Jemmy, My Gramps was Jeremiah."

"And you're Fitz."

Still holding one hand I laced the other hand around her back to pull her closer. "Fitz. My full name is ridiculous but my last name is Deir. I'm the adoption director at the Humane Society. I love animals, Mexican hot sauce and would like a chance to fall in love with you."

Dropping my hand she threw her arms around my neck to pull me close. "Evangelina Grace McConnell. I'm a preschool teacher, I love Vietnamese hot sauce, historical romances, and think I could fall in love with you."

My mouth found hers, the taste of apple cider on her tongue as we kissed. Pulling her flush with me, I could feel the warmth of her body through all our heavy layers.

My hand moved from her waist to the front of her coat. I fumbled with the buttons, trying to get the loose so I could touch more of her. My mouth moved down her throat and she tilted her head back. I got the top button loose and moved her scarf out of the way to kiss her collarbone.

"Why are you wearing so many clothes?' I grumbled against her skin.

She chuckled, a warm sound that heated me. "It's December. Maybe we should move to a warmer spot where we won't get arrested for public nudity?"

With my hand in her hair, I pulled her in for one last kiss before taking her hand in mine.

Constant rainfall is common in the area. Heavy, not so much. The downpour caught us three blocks from my house. Holding tight to her hand, we ran through the slick gray streets towards my bungalow. Water was dripping down our backs and soaking through her coat. Lina's hair was flattened against her head and black smears appeared under her eyes from her makeup. Laughing together, we climbed the three painted white steps of my bungalow.

This time I was smoother. I didn't fumble with my keys as we walked into the house together. I think we both knew that we had all the time we needed.

Coming into my home, Lina wasted no time shedding her coat where it fell onto the bamboo floor with a splat. I toed off my boots, kicked them into the corner. Mud and rain footprints followed behind us as we moved to the bathroom. Lina's teeth were chattering together as I turned on the hot water of the shower. As the water heated up, I turned to face Lina. Her arms wrapped around herself as she watched me through rain darkened eyelashes.

Her dress was red silk, so wet it looked almost black. I realized with surprise it was the same one she wore the night we met. Had it only been six weeks since then? I felt like my entire world shifted that night. I was a different man with her in my life.

Teasing the strap off her shoulder, I bent down to kiss the cool skin as her dress slid down. It was harder to take off the second time around, sticking to her wet skin. She moved her body with me as I eased the dress off her skin. Every inch that I exposed I left a kiss. Kneeling before her, I looped a finger through each side of her thong, bringing it down her thighs. I kissed her hip, her pubic bone, the small mole where her thighs and the apex of her mound met. Her hands in my hair, she sighed as I moved down her body. I wanted to do more, but I couldn't have her cold. Taking every last ounce of willpower I had, I pulled away, rocking back on my heels.

"Get in." I motioned to the shower.

Complying, she got in, watching me disrobe through the steam. Her arms wrapped around herself as she stood in the hot water.

As I stepped into the shower, she moved so that I could stand under the water with her. I shook my head, moving her back under the warm stream until her teeth stopped chattering. "You get warm first."

She ran a cool hand up my chest, her fingers teasing my nipple before cupping the back of my neck. "I was so cold before."

"But you're not anymore?" I asked breathing in the sweetness of her warming skin. I bent down to suck that little spot where her throat meets her collarbone into my mouth.

"Now I'm burning up." Her words throaty as my hands wandered down her body. In the heat of the shower, our bodies were slick together. Grabbing behind her knee, I pulled one leg up until it wrapped around my hip. I leaned against the cold tile of the shower, her leg hitched up around me, her smooth heat rubbing against my cock.

"I don't have a condom in here," I breathed out as she ground herself on me.

"I have the implant." She pulled away, studying me. "And I got tested after my last boyfriend."

I shook my head, amazed that she would trust me with this. At my last check-up, six months before, I had the doctor run tests as well. I knew I was good to go, but she couldn't know that. "Are you sure? We don't have to. I want you to be comfortable. I can make you feel good without those risks if you want to wait."

She shook her head. "No. I trust you." She blinked the water from her lashes as the words sunk in between us. "I want this, you. There's never going to be anyone else that makes me feel this way."

There were no words. I poured everything I was feeling into my kiss. Searing into her how much I missed the feel of her body against mine, the way I needed to see her face in the morning and how I kissed her at night. Into the kiss, I gave her everything I had. Reaching between us I positioned my cock at her entrance, pushing in.

Thrusting into her I gave her all the love she brought me. Her body around me, her slick heat covering me, we were one. Never had I felt more powerful and vulnerable at the same time. Reaching between us, I circled her clit with my finger, timing my thrusts with my hand to get her to orgasm. Already I could ready her body and give her what she needed. Pulling my head back I watched her as I moved inside. With every thrust I was taking her closer to climax. I could tell by the little hitches in her breath and the way her body spasmed around me.

"That's it." I coaxed. "Give it to me. Show me how good it feels to be fucked by the man who loves you."

It was the first time I said the words outright, but I knew it wouldn't be the last. I felt her walls squeezing my cock and I gritted my teeth, holding back until she reached her pinnacle. As she cried out and began to fall, I let myself go, coming inside her.

She fell against my body, heavy from the orgasm. Holding her in place, I let her leg drop down.

Her breathing was ragged as she slowly opened her eyes. "That was..."

Cupping her cheek with my hand I brushed a thumb over the corner of her lip. "It's always going to be like that for us. You and me. This is it. Since that first night, I tried to tell myself that you couldn't be this good, didn't feel so right. But you're better, we're better."

A small smile ticked up on her mouth. "We are, aren't we?"

She pulled my face down to press a sweet kiss to my lips. Wrapping my arms around her body I held her close until the water ran cold.

Warm under the covers in bed, we could hear the fireworks going off over Freedom Bay, signaling in the new year. I knew that next year we would be out on the streets watching the whistling booms as they exploded over the water in a cacophony of colors. We would spend the night with our friends and eventually the family we made together. But this night was ours. This year, this kiss, this new beginning.

JACKPOT QUESTION
Lina - 364 days later

The sound of the front door slamming made me stick my head out of the bathroom door where I was trying to put on a pair of complicated earrings. "Hey! Took you long enough, we're meeting Zoya and Milo in..."

My voice trailed off as Fitz appeared in front of me, holding his hands awkwardly behind his back. I narrowed my eyes at him. Since we moved in together six months before, he had taken to bringing home all sorts of kitschy Viking decor from town. We had five horned helmets, a painting of a Viking gnome, and a replica of a ship. "What did you get this time?"

"Evangelina Grace McConnell..."

"Jeremiah Fitzgerald Deir..." I parroted back as I turned to the mirror to clasp the earring in my left ear.

He shook his head at me. "Lina. Close your eyes."

Setting my loose earring down on the counter, I closed my eyes.

"Face me and put your arms out, palms up."

I opened one eye. "Fitz—"

"Do it, Lina."

I complied, holding my arms out in front of me. There was an odd snuffling sound and then I felt something warm, soft and heavy on my skin. I opened my eyes to find Fitz supporting a wiggling caramel-colored puppy in my hands.

"Fitz." I breathed out. Scooping the puppy against my chest, the dog wriggled around. "He's beautiful. She? He?"

"She's a girl. We have a whole litter that was surrendered a few days ago, but when I saw this beautiful girl, I knew she was ours. Dr. Crosby cleared her a few days ago."

I nuzzled my face into the soft cream fur. "She's beautiful."

He reached over, scratching her behind a floppy ear. "What should we name her?" Fitz asked.

"We have to name her Sriracha." I said, my face still buried in her fur to give her kisses.

"No, definitely not. She's going by Valentina." Fitz said.

"How about Pepper?"

"Pepper, I like that." Fitz rubbed behind the puppy's ear. "What do you think about her collar? Should we get her a new one?"

"Her collar? It looks--" I trailed off as Fitz rotated the collar until I could see the diamond solitaire attached with a blue ribbon.

"Fitz." My words soft. "Oh..."

He was down on one knee, his brown eyes so earnest as he looked up at me. "Lina. I never believed in fate before you, but I know that you and I are meant to be together. I know I want to spend the rest of my life showing you how lucky a man I am that I met you that night. Say yes."

"Yes, I'll marry you." Smiling through my tears. With our new puppy between us, Fitz leaned in to kiss me. His touch as strong as he was.

When we finally made it out to the bar that night, I had forgotten my second earring, but no one noticed because of my new piece of jewelry. There at the bar, surrounded by those who loved us, we toasted to our new beginnings as the clock struck twelve.

THANK YOU

To my wonderful writing friends who cheer me on every step of the way, love and gifs for you. To Kate and Cassidy thank you for reading this story in it's worst iteration and telling me to keep going.

Thank you to my entire family for providing me with a lively debate on the correct way to eat a doughboy. (Although half of you are wrong). To Sluys Bakery for creating the afore-mentioned doughboy. Caitlyn Hatchel, owner of Hood Canal Brewery for answering my brewery related questions.

To my husband, Rusty, for being my biggest fan. And my boys even though I never want you to read this book.

Most of my stories have playlists. This one has a single song. I prefer Ella Fitzgerald's version of Frank Loesser's song, but The Head and Heart has a solid cover. Find me on social media to let me know yours.

ABOUT THE AUTHOR

Linnea March is a contemporary romance author who writes steamy stories about self-confident women and the rugged men who love them. She lives somewhere in the wilds of the Pacific Northwest with her husband, their two boys, and a plump dog. After fifteen years of teaching early childhood education, she put down the googly eyes and picked up a pen. When not writing, she can be found reading her way through an ever-growing pile of books while drinking copious amounts of coffee. She proudly refuses to use umbrellas.

Also by Linnea March

Prevalent Notion Series

Faultless Notion

Treacherous Notion

Ruinous Notion

Reckless Liar

www.ingramcontent.com/pod-product-compliance
Lightning Source LLC
Chambersburg PA
CBHW031544310726
48971CB00008B/2616